THE CONFESSORS' CLUB
CLUB
Jack Fredrickson

Severn

Lon

This first large print edition published 2015
in Great Britain and the USA by
SEVERN HOUSE PUBLISHERS LTD of
19 Cedar Road, Sutton, Surrey, England, SM2 5DA.
First world regular print edition published 2015 by
Severn House Publishers Ltd., London and New York.

British Library Cataloguing in Publication Data

Fredrickson, Jack author.
    The confessors' club. – (The Dek Elstrom mysteries)
    1. Elstrom, Dek (Fictitious character)–Fiction.
    2. Private investigators–Illinois–Chicago–Fiction.
    3. Serial murder investigation–Fiction. 4. Detective and
    mystery stories. 5. Large type books.
    I. Title II. Series
    813.6-dc23

ISBN-13: 9780727872951

Severn House Publishers support the Forest Stewardship Council™
[FSC™], the leading international forest certification organisation. All
our titles that are printed on FSC certified paper carry the FSC logo.

Typeset by Palimpsest Book Production Ltd.,
Falkirk, Stirlingshire, Scotland.
Printed and bound in Great Britain by
T J International, Padstow, Cornwall.

For Jack R. Fredrickson

My guide, my dad

ACKNOWLEDGMENTS

The whole gang – Patrick Riley, Missy Lyda, Eric Frisch, Mary Anne Bigane and Joe Bigane – slogged through the early drafts of this one, criticizing, counseling, supporting. As always, I'm grateful.

Thanks, too, to the ever-patient Sara Porter of Severn House for managing this book, and me, with grace and aplomb.

First, and last, thank you, Susan. Again. For it all.

The gold Rolex Day-Date on his wrist had cost eleven thousand dollars. It was still keeping perfect time, but that would be expected. It was water resistant to a depth far greater than the shallows at the marsh end of the small lake. And it had been engineered to run on the faintest of movements: the gentle lapping of the water through the rushes was more than enough to engage the self-winding mechanism. It was a gentleman's wristwatch, designed for a man who need make only subtle gestures – a wealthy man, a man of nuance.

He had dressed well. His gray gabardine trousers were of the finest wool, light for the warming spring. His white shirt was cut to precise specification, sent over from Jermyn Street in London. His shoes were English as well, lace-up brogues polished by a houseman to a high gloss.

His attire had not fared as well as the wristwatch. The press had gone from the trousers and soft, milky flesh protruded where the water reeds had abraded the wool. The shirt was now a putrid green, mucked by the moss at the shore. And the shoes had puckered and blistered, since even the finest of leathers, no matter how well oiled, are not meant to withstand even partial submersion.

His face, of course, had suffered the worst of

it. The part of the forehead closest to the bullet hole had gone, nibbled away in tiny bites by the sunny fish and microscopic urchins that worked the shore of the small lake.

His eyes, though, still commanded. They remained as clear and direct as they'd been in life, demanding that notice be taken, witness be made, to the truth of the horror they had seen.

One

Amanda called me two days before what would have been our fifth wedding anniversary.

'Happy almost anniver—' I said, before I slammed my mouth shut on words that bubbled up from nowhere. I hoped.

My remembering had caught her off guard, too. 'Dek, how sweet of you,' she said, after an awkward beat. Then, 'I'd like to have dinner.'

We hadn't spoken in months. 'Surely not to celebrate?' I asked.

'Our divorce?' She managed a little laugh. 'Of course not.'

'I'm good all next week, after Monday.'

'Business has come back so well you're not available until then?'

I hesitated for an awkward moment of my own. 'I'm headed out of town.'

'Not business, then,' she said.

'A mini-vacation.'

'Today?' She knew I'd never taken a vacation in my life.

'Not for a couple of days.'

She paused, then said, 'How about tonight? It's important.'

I paused too, but only for a second. 'I'll pick you up. You're still on Chicago's tony Lake Shore Drive?'

'Did you get shock absorbers yet?'

1

'They diminish the aged Jeep experience.'

'I'll meet you at Petterino's,' she said. 'Afterwards, we'll go to the theater. My subscription tickets are for tonight.'

It was going to be like old times, for whatever reason.

'A play afterward?' I managed. 'Surely you remember that's over my head.'

'See you at Petterino's at six.' Her voice softened. 'And Dek?'

'Ma'am?'

'Little is over your head.'

Little was over Jenny's head as well, though her calling ten minutes after I'd clicked off with Amanda could only have been coincidence.

'I can't wait to show you Fisherman's Wharf,' she said.

It was going to be our first time together since she had taken the San Francisco television job eight months earlier. They'd been long months, those eight, and we were set to celebrate the wonder of making our new relationship work at such a long distance.

'Picturesque, is it?'

'Just your cup of Twinkies,' she said.

'Real and authentic, old-time San Francisco?'

'You can get a picture of Elvis on black velvet to hang above your table saw.'

'Black velvet would also nicely complement the white plastic of the lawn chairs,' I said, of the turret's first-floor conversational grouping. 'I'm also in need of a really wide refrigerator magnet, maybe of the Golden Gate Bridge.' The avocado-colored refrigerator I'd found in an alley was rusting from the inside out, and I was looking to slow the loss of semi-cold air.

'I've got four days off, time enough to take care of all your needs.' She laughed, hanging up, leaving me with the promise of unspoken naughtiness.

And grateful that I hadn't had the chance to tell her I was having dinner with my ex-wife that evening.

Two

I've always suspected that a malevolent chicken farmer designed the Goodman Theater complex in downtown Chicago. It's set up like a poultry processing plant. Petterino's is on the corner, a high-glitz restaurant of hooded table candles and deeply cushioned chairs. Good food, big prices. Petterino's is for the plumping and the plucking.

The theater connects through an interior doorway so that patrons, overfed and softly sweating, can be shepherded straight to their seats without being aroused by fresh outside air. Amanda always insisted that the Goodman offers mainstream productions, but to me the plays were confusing. And that, I used to say, is the point. Dulled by overeating at Petterino's, staggering straight into the dim plush of the theater, folks are further numbed by droning actors sayin things that make no sense. The audience sli

3

from stupor into sleep; it's the poultry man's intent. The Goodman is for the lulling.

Two hours later, the audience is jolted awake by the smattering of applause at the final curtain. Groggy, now disoriented by the sudden noise and lights, they're herded across the street to the garage, where they're made to wait in lines to pay a credit card machine that mumbles nonsensical instructions in an adenoidal, digitized voice, then funneled into other lines for a chance to push their way into one of the two overcrowded elevators. By the time they reach their cars, they're dripping sweat, their eyes bright with the need for escape. But the final chaos is yet to come. The automobile exit lanes all merge into one, and the flow quickly becomes choked, an impacted drain, backed up all the way to the roof. Trapped, frantic at the stoppage, the drivers whimper and slap at their horns, but the sudden, overwhelming noise only enrages them further. Control vanishes; it's every chicken for himself. They gun their engines, aim recklessly at imagined hair-width gaps in the line. Fenders crumple, voices scream. It is at this moment that they welcome death. The garage is for the slaughter.

And somewhere, unseen, the poultry farmer laughs.

To me, it is not amazing that people pay great sums to do this. What shocks is that they subscribe to do it several times a year.

Petterino's was crowded with pre-show diners. Amanda, now one of Chicago's wealthiest social-es, had been provided a quiet table in the corner.

4

As she'd said on the phone, she wanted to talk.

I hadn't seen her since I'd dropped her into the welcoming arms of her father, his small army of heavily armed security men and, pacing in front of them all like a silvered peacock, her impeccably attired, suitably affluent new beau.

She looked magnificent as always, in dark slacks, a cream blouse and the garnet pendant I'd given her for her birthday.

I, in my blue blazer and the least wrinkled of my khaki pants, looked like a used office furniture salesman.

We ordered drinks and proceeded carefully. 'How's business?' she asked.

A scandal, stemming from a false accusation, had trashed my business and our marriage. The business was resurrecting, though slowly.

'Two more old insurance company clients are using me again to verify accident information. It's not much, but it's a foot on the road to hope.'

'And the turret?' she asked. We were stilted, awkwardly catching up, but there was something else in her voice. Hesitation. She was stalling, not yet ready to tell me why she'd called.

'I've finished hanging the kitchen cabinets and am awaiting only the funds for new appliances. Now I'm up on the third floor.'

'The master bedroom,' she said. It had never been ours. We'd lived in her multi-million-dollar home in Crystal Waters, a gated community, before my career, our marriage, and then her neighborhood had blown up.

The bed, though, had been ours. She hadn't wanted it, but I'd not been willing to give up.

I'd hauled it from her house before it had been reduced to rubble.

'I've built a closet,' I said, with as much pride as another man might say of a new Ferrari.

She sent a bemused glance toward the wrinkles in my blue button-down shirt.

'I don't as yet have hangers,' I said.

She smiled. 'Of course.'

'Any day now, some hotshot commodities trader is going to drive by, see my five-story limestone cylinder, and buy it for millions. The turret is my other foot on the road to hope.'

Her smile tightened. I'd slipped, seemingly into pettiness. Richard Rudolph, her silver-haired new beau, was a wealthy commodities trader, and precisely the sort of hotshot I was trying to snare.

'You are well, you and Mr Rudolph?' I asked of the hotshot, trying for casual. It had been some time since my friend Leo Brumsky had reported seeing their picture in the papers, always at some appropriately charitable event. I'd supposed that at some point, Leo had decided I didn't need to stay current on such news.

'He's in Russia – new opportunities,' she said, perhaps a little too quickly. Then, 'Jennifer Gale, the newswoman?' Her gaze was direct, her eyes unblinking.

We were catching up more pointedly now. 'How could you know . . .?'

'Your photo ran in the papers too, Dek. Some journalism awards dinner. She's as lovely in print as she is on television.'

Jennifer Gale had been a features reporter for Channel 8 in Chicago until she'd been offered newsier television opportunities in San Francisco. With me, though, she was Jenny Galecki, a sweet, solidly Polish girl struggling to mix celebrity and ambition with feelings for me. For eight months, we'd managed to stay involved, telephonically. And now I was about to head to San Francisco.

'She is lovely, yes,' I said.

For a moment, we let silence shelter us. We'd moved on, some.

I veered away, asked about her work. She'd given up teaching at the Art Institute to establish philanthropies in her father's name. Wendell Phelps, head of Chicago's largest electric utility, had come to regret being an indifferent parent, and had offered Amanda the chance to do really good things with really big money. It was an offer she did not refuse.

'He's moving me into operations. I'm day-to-day electricity now, Dek. I liaise with every city and town on our grid, building relationships. Philanthropy hasn't been on the agenda for several months.'

'He's prepping you for great responsibilities.'

'All of a sudden, he's in a rush.'

'He's the major shareholder. It's prudent to bring his only child into the family business. Lots of investment to protect.'

Our waitress came with drinks – a Manhattan for her; a first-ever, low-carb beer for me. As in old times, we ordered the everything-but-the-kitchen-sink salads that had long been one of the prides of Petterino's.

She stirred her drink for a long minute, and I took a pull from the bottle of de-carbed beer. It

7

tasted like it had been run through something alive, perhaps hooved, to get the carbohydrates out.

She removed the cocktail stick, its cherry still impaled, and set it on the napkin. 'I've told my father to hire you,' she said.

'Whoa,' I said, understanding why she'd played too long with her drink. I set down the bottle of carb-less beer residue. 'Me, work for your father?'

Wendell Phelps was no admirer of mine. We'd never talked face-to-face, but we'd argued plenty on the phone after his daughter had been abducted. His arrogance, along with my stupidity, had almost gotten her killed.

'Actually we've discussed it several times. No, that's wrong. I've brought it up several times.'

'What, exactly?'

'He's hired bodyguards.'

'A deranged shareholder or some nut pissed about his electric bill?'

'He won't say.'

'The business pages say he's taking heat because of all the service outages. The governor and the mayor are pushing him for equipment upgrades, but the big shareholders don't want him to spend the money. It's a real tussle.'

I reached for the low-carb but quickly stopped my hand; drinking more might stick the taste to my tongue permanently. 'I also heard his stock price dropped. People have lost money. Maybe some cranky shareholder got wiped out.'

'He said it was nothing like that.'

'What then?'

She shook her head. 'He won't say, other than

he hired an investigator to take care of it. The man found out nothing, apparently. My father looks old, Dek; old and afraid and weak.'

'Could that have something to do with his new wife?' Long a widower, Wendell's recent marriage lingered only briefly on the society pages before descending into the gossip blogs. The most charitable of them said the bride was charmingly eccentric.

'You're wondering whether she's driven him into becoming delusional? I don't think so. His fear is real.'

'Cops?'

'He hasn't gone to them.'

'What is it with rich people, so afraid of going to the police?' A bomb-wielding extortionist had assaulted the mega-rich homeowners in Crystal Waters, yet none of her neighbors wanted to call the cops. At least not until people started getting blown up.

'He said he'd talk to you.'

'Because if he didn't, you'd hire me yourself, and then he'd lose control of what I learned?'

She smiled a little. 'Of course.'

'No doubt he pointed out I'm a lightweight as far as investigators go, that I research records for lawyers, chase down accident information for insurance companies. I don't do life or death.'

'You did, for me.'

'I got you kidnapped.'

'Talk to him, Dek. Reassure me he's having some sort of small mental lapse. Tell me he's just feeling too many ordinary pressures.'

I smiled then, too, because ultimately that was

what I always did with Amanda. Our salads came, and we smiled through them as well. Our awkwardness was disappearing.

After the play, she told me I'd slept through another magnificent performance. That was too close to old times, too.

Three

Wendell Phelps's house, stone clad and slate roofed, loomed high, a dark fortress on the bluffs above Lake Michigan. To the south, the Chicago skyline was a blur in the gloom of the late March sky, as though it were a backdrop painted pale and inconsequential to make the magnificent mansion stand out even more. Down below, past the closely mowed lawn and the terrace of tightly trimmed yews, the lake lapped at the edge of the raked beach, gray and vaguely restless.

One of the doors in the five-car garage was open, exposing the tail end of what I knew was Wendell's old black Mercedes and, alongside it, the lighter-colored fender of something inexpensively American, likely belonging to a live-in housekeeper. I drove past the garage and stopped behind a dark brown Nissan pickup truck.

A young woman in her early twenties, wearing a brown sweatshirt that matched the truck, was picking shredded yellow flowers out of the concrete urns at the base of the front steps. Large money bought that; fresh flowers before spring.

I got out of the Jeep and smiled at the girl, one tradesperson to another.

'Pigs,' she said, jamming the ruined blooms into a paper yard-waste bag.

'Ah, but they pay the bills,' I said, and walked up the stairs to the massive walnut door.

Amanda told me once that state senators, mayors and business leaders had been summoned to this house, but the only visitor who'd not been made to wait at the door like a pizza driver was the mop-headed former governor of Illinois, now doing prison time out west. Go figure, she'd said, laughing.

An unremarkable man answered the door. Not tall, not short; not dark haired, not blond; not young and certainly not old. Right down to the faint gray stripes in his bland blue suit, he was indistinct, an average man, a medium all around. The best ones are like that: mediums all around. They don't get noticed in a crowd. Only the slight bulge in his suit, under the left arm, gave him away. He was one of the bodyguards Amanda had mentioned, and he was packing.

I showed him my driver's license. 'Dek Elstrom to see Mr Phelps.'

'You're expected.' He pulled the door open all the way.

The foyer was dark, lit only by four small wall sconces. It was only after I'd followed him halfway across what seemed like a football field of black-and-white tile that I realized the walls were paneled in walnut as thick as the front door. That the head of Chicago's largest electric company was wasting none of the company

11

product at home might have come from frugality. Or it could have come from fear.

The bodyguard knocked on a door, stepped aside, and motioned for me to enter. I went into a library as dim as the foyer. The curtains were drawn. The only light came from a yellow glass lamp on the desk in front of the curtains.

'Mr Elstrom,' Wendell Phelps said, rising from behind the lamp.

I'd seen his face in the business news and, of course, in the oil portrait I'd cut to make a Halloween mask in the last drunken days of my marriage. Those pictures were of a younger and more relaxed man. As he came closer, I saw lines deeper than any sixty-three-year-old should have. He wore golf clothes – yellow slacks to match the lamp, and a green knit shirt with a crocodile on it – as though he were about to go hit a bucket of balls in his foyer. The croc's mouth was open, which fit with what I knew of Wendell Phelps.

'Mr Phelps,' I said.

We sat on opposing sofas without shaking hands. A tan envelope lay on the low plank table between us. The only other thing on the table was a small framed photograph of a little girl holding a blue balloon. The picture might have been of Amanda, but it was too small to tell in such dim light.

'What has Amanda told you?' he asked.

'She said you hired bodyguards, one of which I saw for myself, and that you retained an investigator, who learned nothing.'

'We speak in confidence, you and I? You do not report back to Amanda?'

12

'So long as you're the client, and not her.'

He frowned at the reminder of his daughter's threat, and pushed the tan envelope an inch toward me. 'There have already been three murders.' His hand shook a little as he lifted it from the envelope.

There were three letter-sized sheets in the envelope. I held them up to catch the faint light from the desk. They were photocopies of obituaries from the *Chicago Tribune*, the big, quarter-page kind that ran with photographs when someone important died. Each of the three dead men had been prominent in Chicago business. The first had died of a heart attack the previous October, the second from cancer two months later, in December. The most recent had been the victim of a hit-and-run in February, just the month before. None of the obituaries implied murder. I slipped the three sheets back into the envelope and set it on the table.

'They were murdered,' he said.

'Did your investigator tell you this, or is this a hunch?'

'That man was ineffective, and I try never to rely on hunches.'

'Two deaths from illness, the third from a hit-and-run. Not the stuff of foul play.'

'They were CEOs of major corporations.'

His eyes seemed steady; his focus appeared good. Yet he seemed to be speaking gibbered paranoia.

'CEOs die just like ordinary people,' I said.

'They were murdered,' he said again.

'Because they were CEOs?'

13

'Don't patronize me, Elstrom.' He turned around to look at the heavy curtains. A thin sliver of light, half the width of a pencil, shone where the two fabric panels did not quite meet. He got up and went to pull them together.

'Yes,' he said, remaining by the curtains as though worried they'd open again on their own. 'I believe they were killed because they were CEOs.'

I stood then, and walked to the desk. Another tiny picture frame had caught my eye. 'For what motive?' I asked, picking up the photo.

It was the same as the one on the plank table: a little girl holding a blue balloon. I wondered whether it was the only childhood photo he had of Amanda.

'I'm hiring you to find that out,' he said.

'To keep your daughter from nosing into it?'

'She need not worry about this.'

'A plot to kill major business executives would surely interest the brass of the Chicago Police Department. They'll investigate for free.'

'A man with my links to the business community would lose credibility if such accusations were seen as unsubstantiated, or worse, just plain crazy. The effect on my shareholders would be disastrous. Gather sufficient information, Elstrom, and then I'll go to the police.'

He handed me a folded check from the pocket of his golf shirt. It was for two thousand dollars.

It was too big a retainer to indulge what seemed like a rich man's delusion, and it was more than I'd made in the last two months. I put the check in my pocket.

He reached to pinch the seam in the curtains,

though no light was coming through. Whatever the man's tensions were, they were very real to him. I took the manila envelope and showed myself out into the hall. The Medium Man was waiting, and together we made footstep echoes across the marble to the front door.

The flower girl had almost finished replacing the shredded yellow blossoms with vibrant, dark red blooms. I winked at her as I came down the concrete stairs.

She frowned. 'Pigs,' she said.

Four

The Bohemian's offices are on the top floor of a ten-story rehabbed yellow brick factory on the west side of Chicago. The ancient wrought-iron elevator doors opened right into the reception area. Earnest-looking bond and stock-fund sales-people, wearing good suits and carrying thin atta-chés, sat on the green leather wing chairs and sofas, studying the proposals they were about to pitch to the Bohemian's staff of financial advi-sors. I crossed the red oriental carpet to the black walnut reception desk.

'Dek Elstrom, wondering if I might have a moment of Mr Chernek's time.'

The receptionist was new, a tanned brunette at least a decade shy of murmuring the word 'Botox.' She flashed a perfect white smile. 'Do you have an appointment, Mr Elstrom?'

I shook my head. 'If you would just ask?'

'Certainly, sir.' She pushed a button on her telephone console and said my name with a question mark into the thin mouthpiece of her headset.

Behind me, I thought I heard the uneasy shifting of good wool. The tailored suits had sensed a sudden intrusion of polyester. Though my blue blazer, with but the merest hint of mustard on the left cuff, had a forty-five per cent wool content, a blend is a blend, and was as out of place in that reception area as a bongo drummer at a chamber recital. Even the grandfather clock in the corner seemed to stop ticking, anticipating my swift dispatch.

Buffy, the Bohemian's frozen-faced, helmet-haired assistant, materialized in less than a minute to hold the door open for me. And a woman in one of the green leather chairs behind me sighed.

In a different life, I couldn't have gotten into Anton Chernek's offices to wash the windows. He's an advisor – a *consigliere* to Chicago's most prominent families, the ones whose names adorn the city's museums and parks, endow its philan-thropies, and attend its most fashionable events. I imagined his financial counseling was straight-forward enough – the usual recommendations on blue- chip stocks, bonds, mutual funds and such – but it's his role as the go-to guy for other, touchier concerns that defines his real value to the city's ruling elite. When a problem arises that cannot be handled traditionally – a divorce arising from the gamier appetites of human behavior; a scion caught cheating at a prestigious university; an embezzlement within a family firm – the rich

16

summon the Bohemian. He is wise and he is discreet. He makes problems go away quietly, with smiling assurances, packets of cash and, if need be, swift retribution.

We first met when he accompanied Amanda's lawyers to our divorce settlement conference. He'd liked that I'd brought no lawyer and no demands. Months later, he hired me to uncover who'd begun blowing up houses in Amanda's gated community. The case got more gnarly when Chernek was accused of embezzling from his clients. The charge was false, but he was publicly humiliated, and that cost him most of his staff and, for a time, many of his clients.

I knew about false accusations, so I didn't pile on. I kept on reporting to him as though nothing had happened. He never forgot that, or the fact that I never hit him up for freebie financial advice about how to manage the 250 dollars I'd rat-holed in a passbook savings account.

'*Vuh-lo-dek*,' he boomed from behind his carved desk, stretching the two syllables into three. I'm named for my grandfather, a handle that charmed the Bohemian the first time we met. He's been the only one. Not even an animal used to extract carbohydrates from beer should be named Vlodek.

I sat in one of the burgundy leather guest chairs. The Bohemian was around sixty, and a big man, just shy of my six feet two. Today he wore a pale yellow, spread-collar shirt with a figured navy tie that perfectly matched the color of the custom coat hanging on his antique mahogany coat rack. His teeth gleamed; his tan glowed. Not a single combed-back silver hair was out of place.

'You're prospering, Anton,' I said.

'Times are fine, Vlodek. And you?'

'Improving.' I handed him Wendell Phelps's tan envelope. 'I'm interested in these three men.'

He removed the photocopies. He might well have been on retainer with the men whose obituaries he was now reading, but his face betrayed nothing. The Bohemian respected confidences, even with the dead.

'Fine businessmen, in the heavy cream,' he said, looking up. 'Right up at the top with your ex-father-in-law.' He leaned forward slightly. 'Why do their deaths interest you?'

'A client is wondering if anything about those deaths was overlooked.'

He nodded, respecting my need to maintain confidentiality. 'How may I help?'

'How well did you know these men?'

He eased back in his chair. 'Two of them quite well. The third, Grant Carson, the one who got killed by a car last month, I'd met only at social functions.'

'Have there been rumors about their deaths?'

'None that I've heard. It was no surprise that Benno Barberi died of a heart attack last October. His friends knew he had a bad heart,' he said. 'Jim Whitman's death last December came after a long illness, also as the *Tribune* said. That's true enough, as far as it goes, but technically his was a suicide. Jim was dying, and he swallowed all his painkillers at one time. The papers had the decency not to print that, though it's widely known. As for Carson's hit-and-run, you'll have to check with the police. They haven't found the

18

driver, but I don't believe they saw it as anything other than a tragic accident.' He slipped the papers back into the envelope. 'How is Wendell Phelps, Vlodek?' His smile had become sly, venturing a guess about who had hired me.

I gave back just enough of a grin to keep him wondering. 'How many men in Chicago are like these three?'

'Of their stature in business? Off the top of my head, I'd say perhaps fifty.'

'May I have a list?'

The Bohemian's eyes worked to get behind my own. 'You'll keep me apprised?' Meaning that I'd alert him to anyone I thought might be in trouble. Client safety was always his major concern.

'Of course.' It was a necessary quid pro quo.

'I'll email names,' he said.

Five

Traffic was backed up solid on the outbound expressway. No matter the years of supposed improvements, the Eisenhower is almost always a crawl. In my darker moments, I let myself think a secret cabal of oil and communications executives engineered it that way, to trap drivers into burning up expensive gallons of gasoline while raging on their phones, burning up cell-plan minutes. Like my Goodman Theater imaginings, it's baloney – a poor man's cranky fantasy and flimsy as a cobweb – but ever since the Jeep's radio got boosted, it's given my mind something to mull when I'm stuck on the Ike.

I wondered if that sort of paranoia got notched up inside Wendell Phelps. The *Tribune* had seen nothing suspicious in the deaths of Barberi and Whitman, nor had they reported Carson's death as anything more sinister than a typical hit-and-run. More calming was the Bohemian's ear. It was finely tuned, and he kept it pressed to the ground, yet nothing about the three deaths had tripped his sensors. Likely enough, Wendell Phelps had given me nothing more than a dark delusion, except his came with the money to pursue it. Me, I had to get stuck in traffic, sucking auto exhaust, to indulge mine.

I got back to Rivertown as the dying sun began turning the turret's rough limestone blocks into a hundred soft shades of yellow, orange, and red. My narrow five story cylinder is always beautiful at sunset, with its shadows and fiery colors, marked hard here and there with the black stripes of the slit windows, but it can be melancholy then as well, a slim monument in dying light to a dead man's dead dream. The turret was my grandfather's fantasy. A small-time bootlegger with big-time plans, he built it as the first of four that were to connect with stone walls to form a grand castle on the bank of the Willahock River. The one turret was all he got built. He died broke, leaving behind only a corner of his dream.

I walked down to the river to count leaves. When I'd moved to the turret on the first of a November several years before, out of money and out of hope, the spindly purple ash growing alongside the water had already turned its expected autumn purple color and seemed healthy enough. The next July, after a normal spring, it suddenly shed its leaves. By then, that summer had already gone bad. My records research business was struggling to survive and I was trapped in a seemingly hopeless bomb and extortion case that I could not puzzle through. I took the hollow clacking noise the dying ash's branches made, in the wind, in the night, as one more sign the world wasn't spinning right.

I didn't need new signs of bad times. When the next new spring came and the other trees along the Willahock began budding and my ash still resembled nothing but upright kindling, I went out with a pole saw. Better to cut it down than to suffer its death rattle in the night any longer.

I started at the top, sawing and pulling, until all of its brittle upper branches lay on the ground. But as I reset the ladder to cut off one of its two main limbs, I spotted the tiniest tendril of green, no longer than an inchworm, protruding from the bark. I don't know trees but I know trying, and I left that ash as I'd butchered it: a dinosaur-sized wishbone, thrust upright in defiance against the sky.

Several years had passed since then, and it was still slow going for me, and for the ash. Yet once again, in this new spring, the tree was unfurling tiny new leaves like little flags of hope. It was only the end of March, too soon to know how many would come, but I kept count as I ha previous springs, as an act of faith. That night, a fresh sprout brought the new spring's total up to twenty-six.

I take my positive omens wherever I can find them.

I spent two hours on the Internet that evening and found nothing to counter what the *Trib* and the Bohemian's ear had concluded. There had been nothing premeditated about the deaths of Benno Barberi, Jim Whitman or Grant Carson. Still, I planned to give the deaths a long, last mull on the plane west to San Francisco the next day, before calling Wendell to tell him I'd be refunding almost all of his money. Though with that, painfully, would go my hopes to replace my leaking refrigerator.

I took a flashlight into the kitchen, laid it in the refrigerator, shut the door and turned off the lights. A pinpoint sparkled next to where the handle was coming loose; air was leaking out there. As I'd told Jenny, such a small rust-through would be easily contained by a Golden Gate Bridge refrigerator magnet.

Happy times – seeing Jenny, and acquiring a magnet – seemed just around the corner as I reclined in the electric-blue La-Z-Boy, also salvaged from an alley, to watch the start of the ten o'clock news.

And then the Bohemian called.

His voice did not resonate with its usual opti-mism. 'I started on the list of names at six o'clock. was fairly straightforward to establish who our ninent businesspeople are, and I was done

22

by seven o'clock. There are forty-six,' he said, then paused. 'No,' he corrected, 'there *were* forty-six, before the three deaths.'

'This afternoon you guessed fifty. Pretty close, Anton.'

'Life is not so much about numbers as it is about percentages, Vlodek. That's why the three deaths are troubling.'

I shifted the La-Z-Boy to full upright and silenced the four-inch television balanced on my lap. 'Percentages?'

'Three is too many.'

'Two of the three were men in their sixties, and ill,' I said. 'The third was fifty-five, not that it matters, and the victim of a hit-and- run. All three deaths seem easily explainable.'

'Remember the heavy cream?'

'You said all three were among the top fifty business people in Chicago.'

'I misspoke. I meant to use the term more narrowly, to define Barberi, Whitman and Carson as being among the very top of the city's leaders, in the heaviest of the cream, so to speak.'

'I don't understand.'

'I just told you there were forty-six top-flight business leaders in Chicago, right?'

'With Barberi, Whitman, and Carson among them.'

'The forty-six was a simple ranking of business prominence. I then filtered that list to include only those individuals prominent in civic, political and charitable endeavors as well.'

'Only those are in the heavy cream,' I said

'Exactly. I got down to sixteen names.'

'Of which three are now dead?'

'That's troubling. Nineteen per cent of the most influential people in Chicago – three of only sixteen – died in the last four months. Mathematically, that's beyond reason.'

Anton Chernek never indulged false alarm. He was too level-headed, too grounded. And almost always too well informed.

'I'll say again, Anton: two were older and ill. The third, Carson, got whacked by a passing car.'

'Yes, and I was inclined to accept it as an anomaly, an explainable oddity.'

'Exactly—'

He cut me off. 'Arthur Lamm has gone missing.'

'Arthur Lamm, as in head of Lamm Enterprises?' Lamm headed a conglomerate of real estate sales, management, and insurance brokerages. He was very prominent: a political player and a close friend of the mayor. There was no doubt he was in the heavy cream.

'A vice-president of his insurance company told me he's not called in for four days. Do you see what this means?'

I barely heard his voice. My mind was forming the word that I knew he wanted.

'Vlodek?' he asked after a minute.

'Percentages,' I said, giving it to him.

'Arthur's only fifty-one and, from all accounts, he's in peak condition. A marathoner, in fact. If he's met a bad end, he increases your list to four out of sixteen.'

'That's twenty-five per cent.'

He murmured something about emailing me list of names in the morning and hung up.

I needed fresher air in which to think. I went outside to sit on the bench by the river. A small speck lay on the ground, almost colorless in the pale white light of the lamp along the crumbling asphalt river walk.

It was one of the would-be leaves from the purple ash, curled up, stillborn and dry.

Sometimes I don't like omens at all.

Six

I woke at five-thirty in the morning, remembering the Bohemian's anxiety about percentages too much to go back to sleep. I put on jeans, a sweat-shirt and my Nikes and, stepping around the duffel that lay on the floor, still to be packed for California, I went downstairs.

The Bohemian wasn't having a good night either. He'd emailed me his list two hours earlier.

I printed his list, put on my pea coat and took a travel mug of yesterday's cold coffee up the stairs and then the ladders to the fifth floor and the roof. I like to believe I think best on top of the turret. Even when I don't, the dawn likely as not serves up a spectacular sunrise, and that's a good enough reason to go up on any roof at the end of the dark. I leaned against the balustrade sipped coffee and looked out across the spit c land at Rivertown, waiting for the cold caffe and the chilled, pre-dawn air to rouse me f a sleep that never much was.

25

The town was softly shutting down. The tonks along Thompson Avenue were switching off their flickering neon lights, discharging their last, hardiest customers into the night. The slow-walking girls who smiled into the headlights of the slow-cruising gentlemen were shuffling away too, alone at last. And from somewhere down by the river, the sound of shattering glass rose above the rasping staccato of automobile tires hitting the rub strips on the tollway; a trembling hand had let go of an empty pint. Rivertown was twitching itself to sleep.

The thin hint of orange rising over Lake Michigan was bright enough to read what the Bohemian had sent. He'd drawn a simple grid, labeled it 'H.C.' for Heavy Cream – a wit, that Bohemian, even when troubled. On the left side of the sheet he'd listed the sixteen primo shakers of Chicago in alphabetical order. Across the page he'd made columns for the criteria he'd used to select them: business affiliations, political access, social and civic relationships. He'd assigned letter grades for each person, for each category, like a report card. Almost all of the boxes were filled with an 'A.'

All but two on the list were men. The Bohemian's Chicago, that world of vast money coupled to political and social influence, was still very much a boys' club. The names seemed vaguely familiar in the way that names captioned under society ews photographs often seem familiar. Yet if ked, I couldn't have said what most of the nos in the heavy cream had done to achieve prominence. My own world existed farther

26

down, in the muck stuck to the bottom of what was Chicagoland.

The Bohemian had put asterisks next to the names of Barberi, Carson and Whitman. In the middle of the page, next to the name of the missing Arthur Lamm, he'd first drawn a question mark, then added an asterisk.

Asterisk meant death. It was those four asterisks, those four names out of sixteen, which had kept the Bohemian up in the night.

It was the fifth person on the list, four lines below Arthur Lamm's, who had put me in a trick bag: Wendell Phelps. For that, I now hated the son of a bitch even more than before.

My history with the man was limited. I'd called Wendell's office right after Amanda and I married, thinking it reasonable to introduce myself as the man who'd wed the daughter he hadn't seen in years – and maybe become a hero to my new wife, by effecting a reconciliation between the two.

I never got past the secretary to his secretary. No matter, I thought; there would be time to try again later.

There wasn't. I was soon implicated in a fake evidence scheme, having erroneously authenticated cleverly doctored checks in a high-profile insurance fraud trial. My name flashed dark across the front pages of Chicago's newspapers, there not for the notoriety of the trial, or my sloppiness, but because I was Wendell Phelps's son-in-law. I was soon found to be innocent, but I was guilty of being stupid – and of being Wendell's son-in-law. The publicity vaporized my credibility and killed my records research business. Unmoored, I poured alcohol on my self-pity. I blamed Wendell for my notoriety and found that so satisfying that, with the logic of someone totally lost to alcohol, I spread that blame to Amanda for being my link to him. No matter that she'd been estranged from her father for years. In my twisted, liquored logic, she was a most convenient target, and that was enough for me.

It was too much for Amanda. She filed for divorce and I got flushed out of her gated community – appropriately enough, on Halloween – unmasked as a fool.

I crawled back to Rivertown, the town I thought I'd escaped years before, and into the rat-infested turret I'd inherited from another failed man, my grandfather. Amanda fled to Europe, because she had no good place to go either. As I sobered up, I blamed Wendell Phelps for that, too. No matter that I'd trashed his daughter's life; he could have descended from his executive suite to help undo the damage I'd done.

Amanda and Wendell later reconciled, so much so that he enticed Amanda to quit her jobs writing art books and teaching at the Art Institute to join his utilities conglomerate.

He and I had never had need for reconciling anything. We were done, and that was fine for us both.

Except now he was bringing new breath to old furies. If I misplayed his case, investigated what were delusions too seriously, the press might get wind of it and trigger his public humiliation.

28

Worse, if the Bohemian's fears of percentages were accurate and there really was a murderer out there, targeting Wendell and his ilk, my misplaying the case could get people killed.

Damn the man, Wendell Phelps.

By now, the glow of sunrise had risen above the massive dark shapes of Chicago to touch the top of the turret. Mine is the tallest building in Rivertown, a modest attainment in a town of abandoned factories, huddled bungalows and deserted storefronts. The only grand building in town, a city hall of long terraces, expansive private offices and tiny public rooms, was still in the darkness behind me. It, too, had been built of my grandfather's limestone, but later, by corrupt city managers who saw no shame in seizing most of his widow's land and all of its great pile of unused stone blocks. But those lizards couldn't take the sun, nor change the fact that it always lit the turret first every day. I took satisfaction in that.

I crossed the roof to look down at the river. The sunrise would soon light the butchered, two-limbed ash, causing it to cast a dark, jagged 'V' west along the river path. The shadow would look like a giant, crooked-fingered hex, a Greek *moutza* of contempt, thrust directly at Rivertown's corrupt city hall. I took satisfaction in that, too.

Likely enough, there would be no satisfaction in the direction I was now heading.

Damn the man, Wendell Phelps.

29

Seven

News of Arthur Lamm's disappearance had not yet hit the Internet, so I searched for more information on Grant Carson's hit-and-run, the most recent of the deaths in the heavy cream. There was plenty of speculation over the impact his passing would have on his international conglomerate, but there were very few facts surrounding the hit-and-run, and no suspicion that his death had been premeditated murder.

On a day in early February, just after midnight, Grant Carson had pulled his Lincoln Town Car sharply to a curb, got out and was struck by a passing car. He was thrown twenty feet and died instantly. The police noted that by all appearances it had been an accident: Carson had stepped out of his car without checking for oncoming traffic; a car had struck him. Panicked, the driver sped away. The police were seeking anyone who might have witnessed the accident.

I phoned a dozen of my insurance company contacts to learn who'd carried policies on Carson's life. I wasn't interested in beneficiary information; I was hoping an insurance company's private investigation had yielded more than the few facts the cops had released. It was the kind of work I used to do often, before I got tangled up in scandal. I struck gold nowhere, but got promises that others would ask around.

By now it was eight o'clock in the morning in California. I called Jenny. 'I've got a job,' I said.

'A trip-canceling job?'

'More like a trip-rescheduling job.'

'It's life or death, this case?'

'I'm fearing that.'

'What aren't you telling me?' Her newswoman's antennae had picked up words I'd not used.

'Amanda's father is the client.'

'And Amanda – she's involved, too?'

'Only to have steered me to her father. I'm working for him.'

'We were going to have such an amazing four days,' she said, dropping her voice.

'I know.'

'An amazingly lustful four days,' she said, whispering now.

'Oh, how I'd hoped . . .' I said.

'Oh, how I hope you'd hoped,' she whispered one last time, and hung up.

Mercifully, in the next instant I got a call to change the direction of my thwarted naughty thoughts. It was from Gaylord Rikk. He worked for one of Carson's insurers.

'What's your interest?' he asked.

'One of Carson's rich friends asked me to follow up to see if anything new has been uncovered,' I said, trying for casual.

'Ask the cops.'

'I will. What's the status of your investigation?'

'There is none. We've closed our file.'

'So soon?'

'It's been over a month. The police have no leads.'

'The area where Carson got hit is upscale, full of nightlife. It was only midnight. Surely someone saw something.'

'Only midnight,' Rikk agreed, 'in a late-night district that's full of Starbucks, young bucks and sweet girls.'

'Nobody was headed home after a late last purple cocktail or out walking a designer dog?'

He gave me the sort of long sigh one gives an idiot. 'Remember a few years ago, some young woman hit a homeless guy with her car, knocked him up over her hood and half through the windshield?'

'Everyone remembers that.'

'She drove all the way home with the guy stuck, head first, through her windshield. That was at midnight, too, when there were other cars on the road and people out walking. She pulled into her garage with the poor bastard still alive, his head and upper body leaking fluids into her car. He pleaded with her to get him help. Nope. She left him as he was and went into the house – though at the trial she assured the judge she did come out several times to apologize profusely to the guy for ruining his day, or whatever.'

It was the kind of thing I thought about, up on the roof in the middle of the night. 'The guy finally bled out.'

'The point is that she drove through town with the guy's ass sticking out of her windshield, and nobody reported anything. She got caught only when she asked a few friends over to help remove the body. It was one of them who called the cops.'

'Was is mechanical difficulty that forced Carson to the curb, or was he drunk?'

'Neither. No mechanical problems, other than a right front wheel bent from hitting the curb. His blood alcohol was under the limit. He wasn't drunk.'

'You think he was forced over?'

'And got out mad to confront another driver who'd stopped, or just to inspect his car for damage? Possible scenarios, both of them.'

'Why get out at all? If his car was not drivable, why not call AAA or someone else for help?'

'We don't know. He had a cell phone. He didn't use it.'

'What about paint from the car that hit Carson?'

'No sample was recovered from his body or the smashed-back driver's door. Don't trust what you see on TV. Paint doesn't always transfer. Plus, the point of impact could have been glass or stainless or chrome-plated steel, or the car could have had one of those front-end bra things.'

'One of those vinyl covers yuppies used to put on the fronts of their BMWs to protect against stone dings?'

'You still see one, now and again,' he said, 'though most everybody knows they do their own damage, flapping against the paint. All I'm saying is there are all sorts of reasons why paint doesn't transfer.'

'The cops played it by the book, sent out alerts to body shops?'

'Ideally, but there again, those bulletins work mostly on television. Hit-and-run drivers are ordinary people who freak out. They panic.

stick the car in the garage and don't open the door for anything. After a day or two of dry puking and no sleep, they get the idea to dump the car in a bad neighborhood with its keys in the ignition and report it stolen. It almost always works; the car gets boosted and stripped. Hit-and-run cars never get brought to legitimate body shops.'

'Where did Carson have dinner?'

'Somewhere north, I suppose, near where he was killed. He lives up that way, in Lincoln Park. The payout's being processed, Elstrom. The case is dead.'

I called the Bohemian. 'Any news on Arthur Lamm?'

'Perhaps there's been much ado about nothing. He has a camp somewhere up in the piney woods of Wisconsin. He does the real outdoors stuff: small boat, small tent, eating what he catches swimming in the water or crawling on the ground.' The Bohemian's tone of disgust made it sound like Lamm dined on roadkill. 'Anyway, Arthur has some guy who stops in from time to time to check on the place. He said one of Arthur's boats is missing.'

'Meaning Lamm is off somewhere camping.'

He offered up a chuckle that sounded forced. 'I might be imagining evil everywhere, in my old age.'

I asked if he could put me close to people who knew Barberi and Whitman.

'I'm not just imagining, Vlodek?'

'I like to be thorough.'

'I'll call you back.'

He did, in fifteen minutes. 'Anne Barberi is at home. You can go right over.'

'You told her what I'm looking into?'

'Here's the odd part: I didn't have time. She interrupted, saying she'd receive you immediately. She's anxious to talk.'

Eight

Anne Barberi lived at the Stanford Arms, a tall, upscale gray brick-and-granite building across from the Lincoln Park Zoo. While the upper floors surely provided magnificent vistas of Lake Michigan, I imagined the lower apartments occasionally offered troubling views of coupling chimpanzees, and suspected that those units were equipped with electrified, fast-closing drapes. Even when living the good life along Chicago's Gold Coast, the rich had to be vigilant.

A parking valet leaning against a Mercedes straightened up with a pained look on his face, likely soured by the clatter of my arrival. I thought about pulling in to give him a closer blast of my rusted exhaust, but the thrill wouldn't have been worth the parking charge. I drove on, found a spot on a street four blocks over, and hoofed back.

The lobby was enormous, dark and deserted except for two potted palms and two potted elderly ladies, slumped in peach-colored velvet wing chairs, sipping fruited whiskies. The

35

oily-haired man behind the oak reception counter scanned my khakis, blue button-down shirt and blazer like he was looking for resale shop tags.

'Dek Elstrom to see Mrs Barberi,' I said to the oiled man.

'Photo identification, sir?'

I gave him my driver's license. As he studied it, and then me, the corners of his mouth turned down, as if he were wondering whether the blue shirt in the photo was the same one I was wearing. Such was wealth, I wanted to tell him. Even I didn't know; I had three.

'A moment, sir,' the man said, handing back my license. He picked up the phone, tapped three digits and said my name. Nodding, he hung up. 'Mrs Barberi is expecting you.'

I turned and almost ran into a burly fellow who had noiselessly slipped up behind me.

'Mr Reeves will show you to the elevator,' the oiled man said.

He meant Mr Reeves would show me only to the elevator, and nowhere else. We walked to the farthest of the three sets of polished brass elevator doors and Mr Reeves pressed the button. I stepped in and the doors closed before I could ask which floor was Anne Barberi's.

There was no need. The elevator panel had only one button, and it was not numbered. After a short whir and the merest tug of gravity, the doors opened directly into a rose-colored, marble-floored foyer. A gray-haired woman wearing a lavender knit suit stood waiting. Likely enough, she hadn't strung the jumbo pearls around her wrinkled neck from a kit.

'I'm Anne Barberi,' she said, extending a hand that was as firm and in command as her voice. I followed her to a small sitting room. She sat on a hardwood ladder-back chair; I sat on a rock hard, brocaded settee. Freshly cut yellow flowers sat just as stiff between us, on a black-lacquered table.

'Mr Chernek tells me you have questions concerning my husband's death,' she said.

'I'm afraid they're not very specific.'

'At whose behest are you conducting your inquiry?'

I'd considered inventing a lie, but decided simply to stonewall to protect Wendell's identity. Truths are always easier to remember than lies. 'One of your husband's associates,' I said.

'Within Barberi Holdings?'

'No.'

'Fair enough, for now.' She folded her hands in her lap.

'I understand Mr Barberi had a long history of heart disease,' I said.

'For twenty years, he'd been careful, monitoring his cholesterol, exercising under supervision, watching his diet. At work, he chose very able assistants, young men and women who could shoulder much of the stress. My husband was cautious with his heart, Mr Elstrom, which is why I am interested in what you are doing.'

'I'm merely gathering facts, for now.'

She studied me for a moment, realized I wasn't going to offer more, and went on. 'As I said, Benno kept a tight lid on the pressures of his job. Until the night he died, when he lost control. He

37

came home from a dinner furious, literally trembling because he was so upset. I tried to get him to sit and tell me what had happened, but he would not. He went into his study, and a few minutes later, I heard him shouting into the phone.' She looked down at her hands. She'd clenched them so tight the knuckles had whitened. Pulling them apart, she looked up. 'I found him in there the next morning, slumped over his desk.'

'Do you have any idea who he'd called?'

'I assumed one of his subordinates, but I really don't know.'

'No one thought to question what set him off?'

'Come to think of it, no.'

'Can we find out?'

'Surely you're not sensing something deliberate, are you?'

'I like to check everything out.'

'His secretary might be able to help.' She reached for the phone next to the vase and dialed a number. 'Anne, Joan. Fine, fine,' she said, brushing away the obligatory questions about her well-being. 'I've asked a friend, a Mr Elstrom, to find out something for me. I want to know with whom Benno was speaking on the phone, the night he died. It was about some matter that upset him greatly.' She paused to listen, then said, 'I'll tell Mr Elstrom you'll call him to set up an appointment.' She read the number from the business card I'd given her, then hung up.

'Joan was Benno's secretary for years,' she said. 'She knows things she'll never tell me, but she's always been loyal to Benno. And unlike me, she did think to inquire with whom Benno was speaking the night he passed away. He'd set up a conference call with two of his subordinates. She'll make them available to you.'

She walked me into the foyer and pushed the elevator button. 'It was not like Benno to allow himself to become so upset, Mr Elstrom. I won't ask again what you're pursuing, but I expect the courtesy of a report when you're done.'

I said I'd tell her what I could, when I could. As I stepped into the elevator, it seemed likeliest that Benno Barberi had simply lost control as accidentally as had the driver of the freak passing car that had smacked Grant Carson. But as the elevator descended, I imagined I heard the Bohemian's voice intermingled in the soft whine of the motor, whispering urgently about the certainty of percentages. And by the time the door opened, I almost knocked over the burly Mr Reeves in my haste to get out. I hurried across the tomb-like foyer, silent except for the ancient ladies gently snoring beside their drained whiskies, and out into the daylight.

I called the Bohemian from the sidewalk. 'Any luck on getting someone close to Whitman to talk to me?'

'He was a widower. I left a message, and your cell number, for his daughter, Debbie Goring.'

'She'll call soon?'

'My God, Vlodek, do I detect urgency?'

'I don't know.'

'You've seen Anne Barberi?'

'I just left her.'

'And?'

'Call Debbie Goring again.'

Nine

I was stuck waiting for the Bohemian to set up a call from Whitman's daughter, Debbie Goring. I could do it pacing the planks at the turret, or I could indulge in the illusion of exercise at the Rivertown Heath Center. I chose illusion.

The health center is a stained, yellowish brick pile that used to be a YMCA, back when young people came to work in Rivertown's factories and needed rooms, and running was considered exercise instead of a means of fleeing the police. Nowadays, the health center still has a running track and exercise equipment, and it still offers rooms, though now the equipment is rusted and the rooms are occupied by down-and-out drinkers working only half-heartedly to stay alive.

I knew those foul-smelling, dimly lit rooms. After being flushed, drunk, out of Amanda's gated community, I spent the night at the health center, as vacant-eyed as any of the grizzlies who puddled the upstairs halls. Waking the next morning in a room still damp from the pine-scented cleaner used to mask the death of its previous occupant, I looked up and recognized rock bottom. I moved into the turret, clear-eyed for the first time in weeks, and began inching my way back to life.

I still come to the health club. The exercise doesn't hurt, and the sting of pine-scented cleaner in my eyes and nose is a fine reminder not to slip that far again.

I eased over the potholes and parked in my usual spot next to the doorless Buick. As always, the lot was empty except for a half-dozen thumpers – high-school-age toughs in training – leaning against the husks of several other abandoned cars. I made a show of leaving my door unlocked. There was no sense in making them rip the duct tape from my plastic side curtains only to see that the seats had already been slashed and the radio boosted from the dash.

Downstairs, I changed into my red shorts and blue Cubs T-shirt quietly, pretending not to disturb the towel attendant pretending to sleep at the counter. Authentically, he was even drooling on the short pile of stained towels. Nobody minded; nobody dared use them. As with the Jeep, I left my locker door unlocked. The attendant need not dull his bolt cutters only to see I'd not left my wallet or keys inside.

Normally, raucous laughter from the exercise floor echoed down into the stairwell – chatter from the men in their sixties and seventies, retired from jobs that no longer existed, who came not to exercise but to laugh and sigh and share old stories. Not so today. The stairs to the exercise floor were eerily silent.

I understood when I got to the top. The regulars were all there – Dusty, Nick, Frankie and the others – roosting as usual on the rusted fitness machines like crows on felled trees. But that day, nobody was joking. They were staring across the exercise floor.

'Purr,' Dusty said softly.

'Doo,' Frankie murmured, almost worshipfully.

The others nodded, staring, just as transfixed as Dusty and Frankie. Big, yellow-toothed grins split their wrinkled faces.

Across the floor was a woman. She was no ordinary woman. She was a big woman, a jaw-droppingly huge woman, the biggest woman I'd ever seen. She was at least six-foot eight and three hundred pounds, but she packed no fat. Every ounce of her was perfectly proportioned, solid and muscular. And she was beautiful, with golden skin and long, dark hair. She was stretching and bending with the grace of a tiny ballerina, curving her body in such lazy, perfectly fluid motions that I could only imagine what long-smoldering embers were being fanned into a full blaze in the minds of the exercise room regulars.

She turned, so that her back was towards us.

'Purr,' Dusty said.

'Doo,' Frankie added.

The Amazonian goddess wore black collegiate exercise shorts, emblazoned with the university's name in yellow letters across the rump. Those kind of printed shorts are designed with a gap in the middle letters, to allow the fabric in the center to curve into the cleft of the buttocks, yet still be read as one word. But her shorts, probably a man's double extra-large, were stretched so taut

42

that the name read as two distinct words: 'PUR' and 'DUE'.

I left the old men to the frenzy of their imaginations and ran laps.

Amanda called my cell phone that evening. 'Still in town?'

'Yes.'

'Is that worrisome?'

'Tying up little loose ends, is all.'

'My father said you stopped by.'

'Yesterday.'

'How come you didn't then call right away to say he's delusional?'

'I'm trying to be thorough, dot my "t"s, cross my "i"s.'

'Don't dodge with cheap humor.'

'I report to your father, not to you.'

She took a breath. 'You think there's something to his fears?'

'Probably not.'

'Now I am worried.'

'Don't be. There are just a couple of wrinkles I want to check out.'

'*Wrinkles?*'

Too late, I realized she remembered my hot word. A wrinkle was my slang for something troubling enough to require being checked thoroughly.

I tried to joke. 'The older I get the more I'm like an aging beauty queen. Even the smallest wrinkles demand more attention than they're worth.'

She let it go because she knew I wouldn't say

more. We tried other, smaller talk but it was stilted, like the stuff of two people passing time, sharing a cab. After another moment, I invented an excuse to get off the phone. She didn't try to find an excuse to stop me.

I supposed that, too, was a wrinkle.

Ten

Benno Barberi's secretary called just before nine the next morning. I'd been up since five, varnishing wood trim for the third-floor closet and thinking about men dead in the heavy cream. She asked if I could meet with Barberi's two assistants at one o'clock. I said that was convenient. She said fine.

Barberi Holdings, Inc. was headquartered north of Chicago, in a concrete building sunk low, like a bunker, into the rolling close-cut grass alongside the Tri-State Toll Road. The interior was just as hard – concrete walls and a blue quarry tile floor. The receptionist took my name and motioned me to wait on one of the immense, curved white leather sofas. As I sat, my left blazer sleeve grazed the sofa cushion. And stuck. I tugged it free and turned it for a look. A smashed drop of varnish sparkled next to the spot of yellow mustard I'd forgotten to rub off.

I draped my sticky left arm high on the back of the sofa and used my right hand to leaf through a *Forbes* magazine. The issue featured the 400 wealthiest people on the planet. Their brief biographies were disappointing. None of them had made their fortunes rehabbing architectural oddities.

A young man named Brad came for me after five minutes. He wore a blue suit and had an impeccable haircut. He brought me to a small conference room where another young man, this one named Jason, stood waiting. He also looked to have recently visited Brad's barber. His blue suit was the identical shade of Brad's, as was my blazer. But mine, I guessed, was the only one sporting a shiny speck of varnish and the merest blush of yellow mustard.

We sat at the round table and Brad began. 'We understand Mrs Barberi is interested in the problem we discussed with Mr Barberi the night he died?'

'She told me her husband took great care to control stress, yet that evening he came home very upset about something. She thinks that triggered his fatal heart attack.'

Jason spoke. 'Mr Barberi called me at home; I conferenced in Brad. Mr Barberi was worried someone was making a play for equity in the company's stock.'

'Isn't Barberi Holdings a publicly traded company?' I asked. 'Can't anyone buy its stock?'

Jason's gaze had dropped to the sleeve of my blazer. He'd spotted the varnish, or perhaps the mustard. For a second he seemed to struggle to raise his eyes to focus again on my face. 'How technical do you want me to be?'

'A short answer will do.'

'Yes, BH is a publicly held corporation. Anyone can buy its stock. The night Mr Barberi died, he learned that a company he'd never heard of had acquired an insurance policy on his life. He was afraid the insurance payout would be used to acquire BH stock when he died.'

'And gain control of the company?'

'Hardly.' Jason's eyes had begun to stray again, down to my sleeve, but he stopped them cold and looked back up. 'It would take many, many such insurance policies for that. Still, it was an agitation, and he wanted us to look into the matter.'

'Look into what, exactly?'

'He wanted us to find out who had taken out the policy.'

'Even though such an individual could do no damage?'

Jason looked at Brad. Brad shook his head. 'It's complicated,' Jason said.

'You're thinking I won't understand business talk?' I said, too fast. It was the Rivertown chip that occasionally throbs on my shoulder, reacting to two condescending, over-barbered MBAs. I smiled like I was making a little joke, to cover it.

'Anyone who acquires stock can have a voice at the annual shareholders' meeting,' Jason said. 'Someone who owns a large block can have a louder voice, and that can be disruptive.'

Brad cleared his throat. 'It's pointless, now.'

'Because Mr Barberi is dead?'

Brad nodded.

'Mrs Barberi will not be pleased if I come back

46

empty-handed, so I'll ask again: Did you look into the company that took out the policy on Barberi?'

Jason said, 'As Brad said, it was pointless. Mr Barberi was dead.'

They both stood up. They were concerned about their own futures, not the king. The king was dead; long live the king. And I was an inconsequential interloper with varnish and mustard on his jacket. They walked me to the lobby, went through the charade of telling me to call anytime with more questions, and breezed me out into the sunshine.

Before getting into the Jeep, I took off my blazer to lay it on the back seat to dry. As I opened the door, I happened to look back at the building. Brad, or perhaps it was Jason, was standing in one of the windows at the side of the lobby, watching me.

Or perhaps it was neither, but another well-barbered MBA, taking an innocent look outside. The place must have been lousy with them.

Then again, that was probably just Rivertown talking.

Eleven

There were two messages from Wendell on my cell phone. I returned neither. I hadn't learned enough to dismiss his suspicions outright, or enough to interest any cop.

I called the Bohemian. 'Arthur Lamm?'

'No news might be good news, if he's simply out in the woods, eating insects. Debbie Goring?'

'No news is irritating news. She hasn't called.' Then, 'How common is it for a company to insure the life of the CEO of another company?'

'It's done sometimes when a shareholder makes a big investment in the CEO's company. The loss of a chief executive can be catastrophic to the investment, hence the insurance policy.'

'Is the CEO, whose life is being insured, notified when a policy is taken out on him?'

'Almost certainly, because medical history and perhaps even an actual physical will be required. Plus, CEOs are always in touch with their big shareholders. They need their support at shareholder meetings. Where are you going with this, Vlodek?'

'I have no idea.'

'Do you want me to call Debbie Goring again?'

'No. Give me her address. I'll stop by.'

Debbie Goring lived in Prospect Park, a few miles east of O'Hare airport. Hers was a beige bi-level in an older mix of ranch houses and other bi-levels.

A green Ford Taurus station wagon with its tailgate up was parked in her driveway. A short, squarish, dark-haired woman in blue Levis and a plain black T-shirt was pulling grocery bags out of the back of the car. The T-shirt wasn't long enough to cover the death's head skull tattoo on her lower spine. I parked the Jeep in the street and walked up.

48

'Debbie Goring?' I said.

She straightened up, a grocery bag in each arm, and turned around. Most of her was in her early forties, but the skin around her eyes was deeply wrinkled, as though she'd spent sixty years squinting distrustfully at the world.

'Unless you're from the Illinois Lottery, bringing a check for a million dollars, she's not home.' Her voice was raspy from too many cigarettes.

'I'm Dek Elstrom,' I said. 'I'm not from the lottery.'

'No shit,' she said.

'An associate of mine, Anton Chernek—'

She cut me off. 'I've gotten Chernek's messages. I'm not interested in talking to any more insurance bastards.'

'I'm not an insurance bastard.'

'What then?'

'A freelance bastard, with questions about your father's death. Can I help with the bags?'

She hefted the bags closer to her chest and started to walk towards the front door. Tops of four cereal boxes – two Cheerios, two Cinnamon Toast Crunch – protruded out of the brown bags. Oats and sugar seemed a sensible mix; she must have been a sensible woman. 'Adios,' she called over her shoulder.

'I'm serious about investigating your father's death.'

She stopped and turned around, hugging the bags. 'For who?'

'I can't tell you, but it's not for an insurance company.'

She lifted her chin. 'My father was murdered.'

I held out my arms for one of the grocery bags.

She shook her head. 'There's another bag in the car, and two gallons of milk. And slam the back lid.'

I went back for the bag and the gallons, closed the tailgate and followed her to the front door.

She led me through a living room that smelled faintly of old cigarette smoke. Pictures in gold frames of her with two young boys were on a spinet piano against the wall. 'My boys are six and ten,' she said as we walked into the kitchen. I set the milk and the last of the groceries on the counter and stood by the door as she put them away.

Without asking if I wanted any, she poured coffee into two yellow mugs, nuked them for twenty seconds and, after turning on the kitchen exhaust fan, brought them to the table. She lit a Camel from a crumpled pack and dropped the match in a cheap black plastic ashtray. 'When I heard Chernek's messages on my answering machine, I thought, "I'm not doing this crap anymore."'

'What crap?'

'Trying to get deaf people to listen.'

'About your father being murdered?'

She blew smoke towards the exhaust fan. 'I was in an abusive marriage, Mr Elstrom. My husband took off, leaving me dead broke. My father bought me this house, so I would have a place to raise my sons. He was a very wealthy man, but he expected me to make my own way in the world.'

'Yet he bought you this house,' I said.

'He drew the line at his grandsons doing

without.' She took a long pull on the Camel. 'My father had pancreatic cancer; he knew he was dying for quite a while. He had plenty of time to get his affairs in order. He'd arranged for his stocks to be donated to various charitable causes in which he was involved, and had just finished cataloguing his art collection for museums. That, too, is set to be donated.'

'Nothing for you?'

'Not true.' Her face was defiant. 'Insurance was for me. He told me he had a two-million-dollar life insurance policy, naming me as sole beneficiary.'

'He died from painkillers,' I said.

Her eyes tightened, daring me to say the word.

'Suicide,' I said.

She stubbed out her cigarette. 'No payout for suicide.'

'Bad pain can make anyone desperate for relief.'

'I was his only child. We didn't get along great, but he adored his grandsons. If he'd been in the kind of pain where he needed to end his life, he would have changed his other bequests to make sure I got money for my sons.'

'Still, sometimes pain—'

'Please,' she said, lighting another Camel. 'His pain was being managed. He went to the office every day, kept up his schedule. For him to come home and swallow a bottle of pills is too much to believe.'

'What do you know about the day he died?'

'I was told he got to the office about ten in the morning, looked at his mail, and went out to lunch with his attorney. He had nothing pressing

51

because, by this time, my father had shifted his responsibilities to others within the firm. Like I said, he had plenty of time to take care of things.'

'Time enough to make sure there would be money for his grandsons.'

'You got it. After lunch, he talked briefly to a few of his managers about small things and was driven home about three o'clock.'

'Your father had a chauffeur?'

'A hired driver was on standby for the last months, in case his pills made him woozy.'

'And when he got home that day?'

'He took a nap. According to Mrs Johnson, his housekeeper, he got up at six, watched the news as he got dressed to go out to one of his dinners. He left about seven.'

'Do you know where he went?'

'No.'

'What time did he get home?'

'Eleven-thirty, according to Mrs Johnson. And then he went into his study and died, still in his evening clothes.'

'Not in bed?' It was a wrinkle. I'd always assumed pill swallowers laid down, for the wait.

She'd caught the question behind my eyes. 'At his desk,' she said, a little too loudly.

'There was no note?'

'A pill bottle in his pocket doesn't have to mean suicide,' she said. 'He didn't even pause to take off his suit jacket, if the bullshit is to be believed.'

'A medical examiner must have conducted an investigation.'

She stabbed the ashtray with the Camel. 'Haven't you been listening? What the hell kind

52

of person sits at his damned desk, writes no note, and swallows pills knowing his adored grandsons won't get one damned dime?'

I asked if she knew the name of Whitman's chauffer.

'We can get it from Mrs Johnson.' She looked at the clock on the wall. 'I have to pick up my boys from school,' she said. 'Be here tomorrow morning at eleven. I'll take you to her. She'll tell you about my father and my boys.'

At the front door, she said, 'I'll give you a hundred thousand dollars if you can prove it wasn't suicide.'

'I already have a client,' I said, ethical purity spilling from my mouth like gospel washed in Listerine.

'So you said. And just who the hell is that?'

I shrugged.

She smiled, softening the wrinkles at her eyes. 'Tomorrow morning, eleven o'clock. Mrs Johnson will tell you.'

I walked to the Jeep morally intact, true to my first responsibility, my client Wendell Phelps.

And all the way to Rivertown, I fantasized about what I could do with a hundred grand.

Twelve

The next morning, before heading off to meet Debbie Goring, I drove across Thompson Avenue to Leo Brumsky's house. Leo has been my friend since grammar school. He is brilliant, and eccentric. He makes upwards of five hundred thousand dollars a year authenticating items for the big auction houses in New York, Chicago and LA; he drives Porsche roadsters that get jettisoned at the ten-thousand-mile mark; he wears designer suits when he must, and he dates a beautiful research librarian who is younger and taller but has the same genius IQ. All that could fit him into a rare, high social niche except he lives with his mother in her brown brick bungalow. He has an aversion to anything smelling of social snobbery, and buys his casual clothes at the Discount Den, a place where thirty bucks acquires a whole outfit, so long as one is not picky about color, style or size. Since Leo is barely five feet six inches tall, and weighs a spare one-forty, his casual attire is invariably several sizes too big, and makes him look like a malnourished dwarf with an oversized pale bald head, wearing someone else's clothes.

He is the smartest person I know, but more importantly that morning, Leo knew the art market in Chicago. Likely enough, he knew of Jim Whitman.

I noticed the black BMW as soon as I pulled away from the turret. It was parked on the short road that leads from my street to the dingy string of honky-tonks, hock shops and liquor stores that is Thompson Avenue. It was one of the smaller BMWs, the sort junior pretenders drive until they can afford one of the more dramatic models.

A car parked on the stub road was no oddity after dark; lots of johns looking to enjoy fast,

54

last-of-the-night bargains often linger in that exact spot. Never, though, had I seen a car parked there in sunlight.

Odder still was the speed with which the driver's head slid from view, as if it belonged to someone who did not want to be seen watching me.

I did not continue on toward Leo's. I swung left on Thompson and headed east toward Chicago. The BMW appeared in the rear-view mirror two times, hanging far back, but by the time I got to the health center lot and parked next to the doorless Buick, it seemed to be gone.

Still, to be certain, I went straight into the exercise room. It was too early for Dusty and Frankie and the rest of the regulars to be roosting; too early for the Amazonian Pur Due to be stretching her magnificent bulk as well. Except for one poor soul in stained street clothes sleeping on the barbell press bench, I was alone. I walked to the window that looked out over Thompson Avenue and watched for fifteen minutes. No black BMW came into sight. I gave it up and motored over to Leo's.

His yellow Porsche roadster was parked out at the curb, meaning not only that he was home but that likely he'd already been out. And that might mean, if the fates had properly aligned, that he'd been to the Polish bakery.

I walked up the cement stairs. One of the front windows was open a crack, and the sound of people stage-whispering lustful things came through the screen. I pushed the doorbell button twice, trying to time it between the moans coming from Ma Brumsky's softly erotic cable television program.

'Yah?' the old woman's voice shouted above the fast breathing.

'It's Dek, Mrs Brumsky,' I yelled.

'Who?'

'Dek Elstrom!' I screamed. Leo's mother has known me ever since her son brought me home, like a stray cat, in seventh grade.

She thumped the floor with her cane, almost in time with the thumping coming from the television. Leo's office is in the basement. 'Leo, the UPS man is here,' she yelled above the TV voices.

A moment later, the sound of footfalls came through the window screen, the front door opened and an assault of bright colors appeared behind the screen door. Today's rayon Hawaiian shirt was a medley of chartreuse palm fronds and yellow parrots. It was shiny and huge and hung in folds down his scrawny chest, sagging the parrots into something more closely resembling snakes.

'You working for UPS now?' Leo grinned.

'You've been to the bakery?'

'Nothing wrong with your sniffer.' He opened the door and stuck his head out. 'And it's warm enough for the stoop,' he said, and disappeared back into the dark of the bungalow.

He came out a moment later with a long white waxed bag and two cups of coffee in scratched porcelain mugs. The mugs had been scratched even before Ma Brumsky swiped them from the lunch counter at Walgreen's. When we were twelve, Leo had told me, proudly, that all of his mother's plates, cups and silverware came from Walgreen's. I told him I'd figured that out already, since everything had 'Walgreen's' etched on its handles or imprinted into its porcelain. I didn't mention what he had yet to figure out, that Ma had swiped it all on lunch breaks when she worked downtown, before he was born. Nobody wants to think of his mother staggering away from a drug store lunch counter with a purse full of dirty dinnerware.

Leo knelt so I could take a mug, and then sat down. He slid an end of the raspberry coffee cake out of the bag, pulled a steak knife from the front pocket of blue knit pants that coordinated not at all with the blinding chartreuse rayon, and cut me a slice.

'This coffee cake cost more than your shirt,' I said, eyeing the half-sleeve that drooped almost to his wrist. It wasn't even good chartreuse. It reminded me of stomach contents, perhaps de-carbed.

'I should hope so,' he said. 'I wouldn't put a shirt like this in my mouth.'

For a minute, we ate coffee cake and looked at the row of brown bungalows across the street, every one identical to his, like we'd done a thousand times since we were kids.

'I drove by your place yesterday afternoon,' he said, carving me another slice. 'The Jeep was gone, and the turret was locked up as it should have been, since you're supposed to be in San Francisco, indulging fancies with the luscious Jennifer Gale.'

57

'I'm working on a job,' I said.

'Must be important, if you dusted off Jenny.'

'Wendell Phelps.'

Leo raised his eyebrows. Most of the time, the dark fur above his brown eyes languishes in boredom. But when he laughs, or his enormous intellect charges at something, his eyebrows come alive and cavort like crazed caterpillars across the pale skin of his forehead. The caterpillars danced with abandon now, frenzied with curiosity.

'Yes, I finally spoke to the great man, face to face.' I cut myself a third piece of coffee cake. Chicago is known for its wind; one must maintain ballast.

'He called you?'

'Amanda was the one who called.'

'You cancelled Jenny for Amanda?' He liked Amanda and he'd liked us together just as much as he now liked the prospect of Jenny and me together.

'Postponed, not cancelled.'

'I haven't seen Amanda in the papers lately, with that commodities trader, Rudolph,' he said.

'She didn't seem to want to talk about him, other than to say he's in Russia, investigating opportunities.'

'Did you mention Jenny?'

'I didn't need to. Amanda had seen the photo of us at that network correspondents' dinner.'

'The one where you're wearing that cheap, too-small rented tux?' He laughed.

'I should have tried it on at the rental place. Anyway, Amanda and I are strictly business now.'

'Where did you meet her? Someplace dimly lit?' The eyebrows waited, poised high on his forehead.

'Petterino's, and then the Goodman for a play.'

'Just like old times.'

'Wendell thinks somebody is trying to kill him.'

'Jeez.'

'Amanda is hoping her father is simply stressed, imagining things.'

'But you don't.' He didn't ask it; he said it. Since we were kids, Leo could see into my head like he was looking through glass.

I told him about Grant Carson's hit-and-run and Benno Barberi's fatal heart attack. 'You've heard of these guys?' I asked.

'I recognize the names. Movers and shakers, for sure, though I'm not solid on what they moved and shook.'

'Then there's Jim Whitman.' I eyed the coffee cake, thinking it wouldn't take running but a few laps to justify an incredibly tiny small fourth piece.

'I knew Jim.'

'Actually, he's why I'm here.' I removed a three-inch width, fully intending to get back to the health center soon.

'No doubt,' he said, watching me heft the wide new slice.

'How well did you know Whitman?' I asked through the pastry.

'I helped value some of the paintings he was going to leave to museums.' Leo's eyebrows began to move, restless with a new thought. 'His death wasn't understandable?'

'He went out for the evening, came back, sat at his desk at home and up-ended a bottle of painkillers. It was understandable to the medical examiner, given Whitman's terminal condition.'

'But?' Leo at his most terse is Leo at his most probing.

'His daughter doesn't buy it. His suicide nullified an insurance payout to her, money intended to provide for his beloved grandchildren.'

'I remember Jim mentioning his grandchildren. He was very proud of them. And, for a man facing death, he seemed very businesslike, very much in control.'

'Suicide that nulls provision for his adored grandchildren doesn't sound businesslike.'

'How much?'

'Two million to her.'

'No. I meant how much did Whitman's daughter offer you to prove her father's death was no suicide?' His lips started to tremble with the beginnings of a smile.

'I told her I already have a client.'

The grin widened into a smile that split his lips.

'Damn it, Leo.'

He smiled broadly, exposing eight hundred big white teeth. 'How much?'

'A hundred thousand.'

'All wrapped up around a case involving Amanda.' He raised his scratched Walgreen's mug, satisfied.

'I love quandaries and ethical dilemmas,' he said.

Thirteen

Debbie Goring was leaning against the back fender of her Taurus, smoking, when I got there at eleven. She looked to be wearing the same blue jeans, but her T-shirt that day was orange and had a Harley Davidson logo on the front. She took a slow look at the silver tape curling off the Jeep's top and side curtains like a spinster's hairdo gone wild in an electric storm, flicked the cigarette butt into the street and said she'd drive. I took no offense.

Ten minutes later, we pulled into old streets lined with big trees and what used to be considered substantial houses. Used to be – because the teardown phenomenon was now changing the definition of substantial in Deer Run, her father's town. On every block, at least one huge new house hulked across an entire lot, dwarfing its neighbors.

'Teardowns are big here,' she said, braking as a flatbed truck ahead stopped to unload a bulldozer. 'Any property worth less than five hundred thousand gets pushed over to build something for a couple million or more.'

'That would buy an entire block of houses where I live,' I said.

She backed into a drive and turned the Taurus around. 'People want to live here, for the charm of an old town, but they don't want the modesty

61

of an old house. Better to knock it down, they think, and put up something flashier and bigger in the middle of all that old charm.' She shook her head. 'You should see these new places at night. They've got lights everywhere – under the eaves, on the railings, beneath the shrubs. After dark, some of these streets look to have a whole bunch of starships landing.' She shot me a sly grin. 'All that need for showiness makes me wonder if there's something wrong with their personal parts.'

She stopped in front of a Spanish-style stucco two-story home with a red tile roof, across the street from the Deer Run Country Club. It was a nice enough house, but not the kind of place I'd been expecting for a multi-millionaire. My respect for Jim Whitman went up a level.

I looked at her.

'Sure to fetch a half-million as a teardown, if Mrs Johnson sells,' she said, getting out.

'The housekeeper inherited his house?'

'While his grandchildren got nothing.'

We walked up to the front door and she rang the bell. A minute later the door was opened by a trim older woman in gray pants and a black sweater. The woman smiled.

'Hello, Mrs Johnson.' Debbie's voice had turned soft and I wondered if the butch rasp she'd been using, talking to me, was an act for when she felt threatened. She introduced me to the housekeeper and we walked into a cool central hall.

The living room had a brown glazed tile floor and mission-style, black metal windows. Lighter rectangles on the beige stucco walls showed where pictures had recently been removed. Several cartons were stacked in the corner. We sat on wide, well-worn, nubby fabric chairs.

'Forgive the mess,' Mrs Johnson said to Debbie. 'I'm boxing up the last of the bequests he left to the museums.' She said it almost apologetically.

'Thank you for seeing us,' Debbie said.

Mrs Johnson reached to squeeze Debbie's wrist, and turned to me. 'I understand you're going to help with the insurance.'

I nodded. It saved me from explaining I had another client who was seeing murder. 'The day Mr Whitman died, he came home in the middle of the afternoon, took a nap, then watched the evening news as he dressed to go out?'

'Yes,' Mrs Johnson said.

'How were his spirits?'

'The usual, no worse. Mr Whitman tried not to let his troubles show.'

'Did he appear to be in pain?'

She pursed her lips, thinking back. 'No. His pills seemed to be working as always.'

'What time did he go out?'

'At seven. Mr McClain, his driver, came by early and we had coffee in the kitchen while Mr Whitman finished getting ready.'

'Do you remember where Mr Whitman went that night?'

'I'm sure it's written in his appointment book. Is it important?'

'I like to get all the details.'

'Let's find out, then.' She stood up and Debbie and I followed her down the narrow stucco hall to a small study lined with bookshelves. The Spanish motif of the rest of the house had been continued in the carved mahogany desk and the tooled red leather reading chair.

'I've thrown nothing of your father's away,' Mrs Johnson said to Debbie as she picked up a blue leather planner from the desk. She opened the book, flipped the pages to the back. She stopped at December thirteenth. It had been a Tuesday.

I looked over her shoulder. 'What is "C"?' I asked.

She shook her head. 'I don't know. Mr Whitman abbreviated everything,' she said, slowly fanning a few more pages so I could see.

The pages were filled in with one- and two-letter abbreviations. For someone dying, James Whitman was a busy man.

'Most of them I can decipher,' she said, looking down at the book, 'but "C" has me puzzled.'

'His driver would know where he took him.'

'Of course, especially since that was the night Mr Whitman died,' Mrs Johnson said.

We went back to sit in the living room.

'How did Mr Whitman seem when he came home later that evening?'

'Very fatigued, but he tired easily, the last few weeks. I was putting away some things in the hall closet when I heard the car pull up. I'd been listening for him because he was out later than usual. I looked out, saw him get out of a different car—'

'A different car?'

'Mr McClain usually drove a black Cadillac,

but that night he brought Mr Whitman home in a tan-colored car,' she said. 'When Mr Whitman came in, I asked him if he needed anything. He said he was tired and was going to get something in his study and then go to bed. I said goodnight and went upstairs.' She pulled a tissue from the pocket in her pants.

'Do you have a card for Mr McClain?'

'I have his telephone number memorized,' she said, reciting it.

I wrote it down and asked, 'You were the one who found him?'

'The next morning. He was always an early riser, even at the end. I made coffee, and brought a cup for him to the study. It was then . . .' Her voice trailed off as she touched the tissue to her eye.

It was all so eerily similar. Anne Barberi had also found her husband dead in his study the morning following a night out.

'What medication, exactly, was Mr Whitman taking?' I asked.

She glanced at Debbie, then back at me. 'You mean, what did he use to end his life?'

'Yes.'

'Gendarin. I'll get it for you.' She got up and left the room.

Debbie turned to me. 'Why is the kind of pills important?'

'It's only a detail for now, nothing more.'

The sound of a cabinet door opening and closing came from upstairs, and then Mrs Johnson came back into the room and handed me an orange vial. 'Gendarin, as I said.'

The vial was full. The label said it contained twenty-eight pills, to be taken one every twelve hours. It was a fourteen-day supply.

'These haven't been touched.' According to the label, the prescription bottle had been filled a little less than two weeks before Whitman died.

'This wasn't the vial they found in his pocket,' Mrs Johnson said. 'This was to be the new supply. He always reordered when he opened a new vial. That way, he always had a full two weeks in reserve, which I kept upstairs.'

'This was the only Gendarin he kept in reserve?'

'It's a controlled narcotic. They won't let you buy too much. I was to pick up a new refill when he began taking pills from this one.'

Something about what she'd just said flickered in the dark attic of my mind and disappeared.

'He carried the current vial he was using?' I asked instead.

'Always. The police made much of the vial they found in his pocket, but I told them he didn't want to risk being someplace without his pills.'

'He occasionally took extras, when the pain got severe?'

'Not that I know of. Carrying the pills was mostly a precaution.'

'Do you know where that vial is now?'

'I imagine the ambulance people took it.'

Debbie leaned forward in her chair. 'My father would not have left me without insurance.'

'Of course not,' Mrs Johnson said, shifting to look right at me. 'Mr Whitman was a meticulous

66

person. He had his insurance man over here several times in the last year, going over this and that. He wanted to make sure everything was in order.'

The room went quiet. Both women leaned forward, attentive, anticipating, as though I might pop out a theory that would correct everything. I had no theories. I stood up. Debbie Goring and Mrs Johnson exchanged glances, then got up too.

At the front door, Mrs Johnson said, 'I feel so bad, Debbie. Your father left me a wonderful bequest. I don't have to work again if I don't want to. But you . . .' She reached for her tissue.

'It's all right, Mrs Johnson,' Debbie said. 'Elstrom here is going to set things straight.'

I didn't look at either of them as I walked to Debbie's station wagon and got in.

Debbie got in a second later, started the car and we pulled away. Lighting a cigarette, she spoke in the same small voice she'd used in front of Mrs Johnson. 'That didn't help, did it?'

'I don't know,' I said. I seemed to be saying that a lot lately.

'You won't help me?' she asked, her voice rasping now.

'I don't know how, yet.'

We drove the rest of the way in silence. She pulled into her driveway and we got out.

'I'll call his driver,' I said over the roof of her car, but it was to her back. She was already walking away.

Fourteen

The main drag through Deer Run was noisy with traffic. I pulled into a cemetery, parked next to a granite Civil War sentry who looked like he might welcome company, and called the chauffeur's number. Robert McClain answered on the first ring. He sounded eager for company, too, but said he played bridge until three o'clock. I told him I'd see him then.

I hadn't eaten since the modest half of a long coffee cake at Leo's. I drove into Deer Run's business district, hunting for a fast-food restaurant with the right kind of windows. I got lucky right away. A storefront across from the train station was papered with window banners advertising chili dogs, half-pound hamburgers and cheese fries. The promise showed in the sharpness of the red letters on the white signs. They were not sharp. They were blurred. I cut the engine and got out to make sure. Right off I spotted a fly stuck to the inside of the window, proof enough that the faintly fuzzy signs weren't the result of sloppy brush work. The blur came from the glass. I went in.

Kings, Kentuckys and Macs are never my first choice because their windows are invariably spotless. The joints I seek have glass made opaque by the inside air. If the windows are filmy with grease, the chef is using properly fatty meat and real lard – sure signs he's not cooking to some bland, committee-crafted, offend-no-one formula. I see it as my obligation to support such efforts by visiting those grease blots as frequently as I can, for they are highly flammable and regularly explode into black smoke.

I ordered a hot dog, onion rings and a Diet Coke and took them to a Formica counter to look at the blur of the world outside. My first bites validated my greasy window theory once again. The hot dog was properly slippery, topped with pickle, tomatoes, peppers, mustard, chopped onions, dill salt and absolutely no trace of catsup. The rings were strong, sure to delight for the rest of the afternoon. And the Diet Coke . . . well, the Diet Coke, like every diet soft drink, was there simply to dissolve calories.

I puzzled again over my earlier sense that I'd missed something when Mrs Johnson talked about Whitman's pills. And in a moment, I had it: Whitman had been about to crack open the reserve vial of pills she'd showed us. That meant his current supply, the one they found in his pocket, should have been almost depleted if he'd been taking his pills in the dosage prescribed.

I swallowed the last bit of hot dog and turned around to ask where the police station was. The man behind the counter shrugged and said something in Spanish to the woman who'd taken my order. 'Three blocks up the street,' she said. 'It's in the basement of City Hall, opposite the park.'

I stepped almost lightly outside, sure of my

wisdom in selecting a hot dog and onion rings for lunch. Like an automobile, my brain functions best when it's freshly greased.

I decided to hoof the three blocks. Crossing the first street, I spotted a junior-grade black BMW parked down the side street, just like the one that had tailed me for a time earlier that morning. I continued on to the middle of the next block, and stopped as if to look in a store window. No black BMW or well-barbered head on feet had followed.

Deer Run's city hall was red brick and white pillars. Walking down to the police department in the basement set the onion rings to barking. I slid three breath tapes into my mouth. The tapes were generic; I get them at the Discount Den in Rivertown, at the same place I get the duct tape to mend the rips in the Jeep's top and Leo gets his shiny Hawaiian shirts and fluorescent pants. I aimed a test breath at the painted yellow block wall before opening the metal door at the bottom. Nothing peeled. Encouraged, I went in.

'I'd like to talk to someone about Jim Whitman's death,' I said to the desk sergeant.

He scooted his chair back a yard, making me wonder if the Discount Den's breath tapes were as unreliable as the duct tape that curled from the Jeep every time it rained. I slipped my hand surreptitiously into my pocket and thumbed loose another tape.

'Your business?' he asked, looking off to my right where, perhaps, there was better air.

I held out a card. It says I do insurance investigations. He scooted forward, grabbed it, and again retreated fast. I slipped the new tape into my mouth.

He frowned as he studied the card. 'I thought you insurance guys closed your file.'

'I'm just filling in a couple of blanks.'

The sergeant swiveled around. 'Finch, get the Whitman file,' he yelled to the empty hallway behind him. Turning back, he motioned for me to sit by the door, on the plastic chair farthest from his desk.

Officer Finch came out in five minutes. He was young, maybe twenty-five, and carried a brown accordion file. 'How may I help you, sir?' he asked.

'I'd like to know how much Gendarin Jim Whitman swallowed the night he died.'

Finch looked to the desk sergeant, who nodded. Finch took a sheet of paper from the file and said, 'Approximately twelve hundred milligrams. It was enough to send him to the moon twice.'

'You're sure it was Gendarin?'

Finch took out a clear plastic bag. Inside was an orange pill bottle identical to the one Mrs Johnson had showed me. It rattled as he held it up to read the label. 'Gendarin,' he said.

'May I?' I asked.

'So long as you leave it inside the plastic bag,' he said, and handed it to me.

The pill bottle rattled again as I held the bag up to the light. 'There are still pills in there,' I said, like I was surprised.

'Two,' Finch said.

'This vial was found in Whitman's suit jacket?'

'Yes.'

71

I read the label through the bag. Just like the reserve supply Mrs Johnson had showed me, this vial had contained twenty-eight pills, eighty milligrams each, prescribed at two a day. It had been filled almost a month before Whitman died. That made sense, calendar-wise. It had been kept in reserve for two weeks before Whitman had begun taking pills from it, at the prescribed rate of two a day, not quite two weeks before he died.

Which meant the vial I was now holding should have contained but a few pills, the end of a two-week supply.

Which meant it could not have contained enough pills to kill him.

'You're sure the medical examiner found twelve hundred milligrams of this stuff in Whitman's system?' I asked.

'Approximately.'

'Isn't it odd that two pills remain inside this vial?'

'Whitman would have known just a few would do the trick.'

I gave him the arithmetic. 'Fifteen pills were needed to put twelve hundred milligrams in his system.'

'OK,' the desk sergeant said slowly, not comprehending where I was heading.

'That's over half a vial. His reserve supply at home was untouched.'

'What are you saying?'

I rattled the vial in the plastic bag. 'He took pills from this vial exactly on schedule, two a day. Where did Whitman get fifteen pills to swallow all at once?'

72

Finch grabbed the bag back. 'From this—'

'No,' I cut in. 'There weren't enough left in there.'

The desk sergeant cocked his head, motioning Finch to leave. 'You'll have to check with the medical examiner,' he said to me.

I gave it up, and walked up the stairs. I took a long look through the window in the door before going out. I saw no black BMW or sharply barbered MBA outside, but I'd just seen plenty inside.

I crossed the street to a drug store and bought a pack of Listerine breath tapes. They were stronger than my generics, and got rid of the taste of onions right away.

But they didn't mask the bile that had risen in my throat.

Fifteen

Robert McClain was in the parking lot behind his dark brick apartment building, dry wiping a shiny black Cadillac Seville. He looked old enough to have been driving when roads were made of dirt.

'I like to be ready, in case I get a call,' he said, smiling.

I asked him about Jim Whitman.

'Working for Mr Whitman was a real pleasure,' he said. 'Most fellows would have insisted on a younger driver, but not Mr Whitman. He was

73

always real polite and regular, always sat up front with me. He tipped really well.'

'Do you remember the night he died?'

'Like yesterday. I knew he was ill – he was straightforward about it – but he didn't act like a man about to kill himself.'

'His spirits were good?'

'Considering what he was facing, yes. As usual, he talked about his grandchildren all the way into the city.'

'You picked him up about seven?'

McClain nodded. 'Went in, had a spot of coffee with Mrs Johnson while Mr Whitman was getting ready.'

'Do you remember where you took him?'

'Corner of Michigan and Walton, downtown.'

'I meant which restaurant.'

'No restaurant. Dropped him at the same corner, as usual.'

'You'd taken him there before?'

'Every few weeks. He never did say where exactly he was going from there.'

'And you picked him up later at that same corner?'

'Not that night. He called to say he was catching another way home.'

'You didn't bring him home in a tan-colored car?'

'This baby's all I got,' he said, touching the gleaming hood of the black Cadillac.

'Was it usual for him to find another way home from there?'

'He'd never done it before. Every other time, I picked him up at ten o'clock sharp. He'd be

74

standing on that same corner, waiting.' He picked up his rag, worked at an imagined spot. 'That was the last time I drove anybody.'

'Business slow?'

'I'm old, and I look it. The agency's got younger drivers.'

There was nothing left to say. I left him in the late-afternoon sun, polishing a future that likely had disappeared.

I busied myself cutting the last of the closet trim that evening. I needed simple work requiring clear and logical steps while my mind stumbled about in the fog surrounding Jim Whitman's pills.

For a time, it worked. The cutting, sanding and staining were calming, easy steps in an understandable sequence. But then, well into the evening, it came time for varnishing. Varnishing, done right, requires care: one pass, no overbrushing. Be too fast, and a spot can get overlooked.

And that's what happened with the cops looking at Jim Whitman's death. They'd missed a big spot: they hadn't accounted for his pills. He couldn't have used his current two-week prescription to kill himself because there had been too few remaining. And he hadn't tapped his reserve vial because it was untouched. He had to have gotten his fatal batch of fifteen pills from a third source.

Unless he hadn't. Someone else could have slipped Gendarin into his meal or his drink, knowing that the excess in his bloodstream wouldn't be questioned because it was the pain medication he was already taking. It would have been assumed that Whitman used his own supply to overdose himself.

What I couldn't see was the logic in risking the murder of an already dying man.

The vague thoughts and the pungent smell of the varnish finally made me woozy. I walked down to the river to sit on the bench and breathe in the cold March air. Behind me, the jukes in the tonks along Thompson Avenue were beating out big bass notes, primitive drums summoning tribe members to return. I almost envied those in that dark carnival. They were sure of what they were seeking: a simple tingle from some booze, a few laughs, a rub of rented flesh.

Perhaps it had been that simple for Jim Whitman, that last night. Maybe he'd finished a good meal, enjoyed a few drinks, had a few laughs being driven home by a friend . . . and realized things would never get any better than they were that evening. Maybe he'd rat-holed a stash of Gendarin for just such a time, and asked himself, on the spur of that moment: Why not? Why not check out with a belly full of good steak and good Scotch, and the sound of a laugh still resonating in the back of his throat? Why not?

Except for the grandchildren he'd left without a nickel.

The dim light from the lamp along the riverwalk made a tiny shadow on the ground just beyond my feet. It was another still-born ash leaf, curled and dried on the grass. I looked up at the tree. There was not enough light to see for sure, but

I knew in my throat that no new leaves had appeared that day.

I took out my pocket calendar and recorded that loss, too.

Sixteen

Two men in loose-fitting gray suits, one carrying a square carton, the other something the size of a wrapped painting, came out of the Whitman house the next morning, heading toward the black Ford Expedition parked at the curb. They stopped when they saw me pull up. The one with the painting gestured at someone in the big SUV, and a third man, also in a suit, got out from the driver's door. All three stood motionless, watching me. I couldn't see the guns, but I knew they had them. Whatever Jim Whitman had bequeathed, it was worth enough to merit three guards.

Mrs Johnson had followed the two men out of the house, saw them tense and stop on the front walk. She turned to look where they were looking. I waved out the Jeep's open side curtain. She squinted, recognized my face. 'We're almost done,' she called. And the world righted itself. The men carrying the box and the painting resumed walking toward the SUV, the driver got back inside, and I settled back to wait.

Ten minutes later, Mrs Johnson followed the armed men out with the last of the cartons, and watched them drive away. She came over to the Jeep. 'You can't imagine how relieved I am that those things are on their way to the Museum of Contemporary Art,' she said. 'The house has an alarm, but I've not been comfortable there, alone with all those valuable pieces.'

'They'll be exhibited soon?' I asked as we went up the front walk.

'The curator said they'll be catalogued, then stored. In a year, maybe less, they'll be rotated into exhibition.'

'How valuable are the pieces?'

'Millions,' she said, as we entered the house. 'Mr Whitman was a plain man, not the usual patron of the arts. Those pieces were recommended as investments. From what I understand, he profited quite handsomely from their purchase.'

'Yet not even one was left to Debbie.'

The distress on her face seemed genuine. 'Wealthy fathers can be especially difficult on young daughters. And Debbie, as you might imagine, was very strong-willed. But Mr Whitman cared for his daughter, and adored his grandsons.'

'You find it odd that he left them nothing?'

'It's impossible to believe. And now you've come back because you're wondering where he got the pills, haven't you?'

'Yes, and I'd like to see his calendar again. You're certain there was only one bottle of Gendarin in reserve?'

'Certain as I can be. As I said, Mr Whitman wanted to keep more on hand, in case the pain got worse, but his doctor wouldn't go for it.

78

Federally regulated narcotics are so very tightly dispensed.'

'Could he have set aside a pill or two from each refill, to build up an extra supply?'

'That's very doubtful. He truly needed those pills, and skipping one would mean going twelve full hours in pain. And yes, Mr Elstrom,' she said, 'I told that to the police, but they didn't seem interested.'

'Any more thoughts on where Mr Whitman might have gone that last night?'

'Mr McClain was no help?'

'He dropped off Mr Whitman on North Michigan Avenue. Someone else drove him home.'

'In that tan car I saw.'

'Any idea whose it was?'

'Only thing I know it was tan, and it was a Buick.'

'You know cars well enough to spot a Buick?'

'Goodness, no. All cars look the same to me these days, like jelly beans. It's just that when I was young, Buicks had those holes . . .' She stopped, searching for the words.

'Like portholes, on the sides of the car?'

'That's it. Imagine Buick still doing those holes, only smaller, after all these years.'

We went into Whitman's study. She picked up the calendar from the desk and handed it to me. I opened it to the page for December 13, the day he died, and looked again at the half-dozen entries. His first appointment was for lunch, at eleven-thirty. Other names were penciled in, beginning at one, ending at two-thirty. After that, the calendar was blank until the 'C' entry, scrawled across the lines for the evening. I pointed to it.

'As I told you last time, I don't know that one,' she said. 'After you and Debbie left, I flipped back a few months. There are other entries just like it.'

'McClain said the same thing. He dropped Whitman at the same intersection, Michigan at Walton, every fcw weeks.'

'You think he got the Gendarin there?'

'I can't understand why he'd need to. He had enough in reserve here to kill himself.'

'I went through the whole house, Mr Elstrom. I found no third vial, no trace he'd hidden more Gendarin.' She studied my face. 'You came back because you're thinking what I'm thinking.'

'Two pills remaining in the vial in his jacket, as there should have been? Full reserve supply upstairs, as there should have been? Leaving us to accept he'd gone to the bother of obtaining the pills he needed to kill himself elsewhere, when he didn't need to? Yes, I'm having a problem understanding why he'd go to that trouble.'

'He didn't commit suicide, did he, Mr Elstrom?'

'I can't prove that.'

'Why would someone risk killing him? Why not simply wait?'

'Did he have enemies?'

'Business adversaries, perhaps, though Mr Whitman was not ruthless, not someone who took unfair advantage.'

I started turning back the calendar pages. 'I need to know where he went that evening.'

The appointments looked to have been written by two different people. Most were in a feminine hand. 'Did you make most of these entries?'

'His secretary made those,' she said. 'The ones that are barely legible, like that 'C' for the night Mr Whitman died, he wrote himself.'

Almost every page had an abbreviation for an evening appointment. I started pointing randomly to different evening entries.

'Y?'

'YMCA of Metropolitan Chicago, usually a dinner meeting for the directors, every three months.'

'MP?'

'Millennium Park, the new park on Michigan Avenue. He donated one hundred thousand dollars.'

I came to another 'C' entry, two months earlier, in October.

'That's one of the others I found,' Mrs Johnson said.

Again it was simple and cryptic, scrawled across the lines for evening appointments. Beside me, Mrs Johnson shook her head, offering nothing. I turned back more pages. There were 'C' entries in August, June, April and February.

'Did he keep another desk diary at his office?' I asked.

'This was the only one; he carried it back and forth in his briefcase.'

'Maybe the prior year's book has more information?'

'His secretary kept his old diaries,' she said, picking up the phone. Then, while she was dialing, 'Why would someone murder an already dying man?'

There was no answering that.

Seventeen

Whitman Industries occupied four floors in a high-rise office building just north of the Chicago River. Jim Whitman's former secretary, a trim, efficient woman in her mid-fifties, came to the lobby carrying two blue leather desk calendars identical to the one I'd brought from Whitman's house. We sat in a secluded corner next to a plant.

I opened the calendar I'd brought to December 13, the night Whitman died. 'Do you know what this is?' I asked, pointing to the 'C.'

'I wondered about those,' she said. 'I wrote most of the appointments in his book, and knew almost all of the ones he entered. But those "C"s . . .' She shook her head. 'I never asked, of course.'

'Were there many?'

'Several a year.' She opened one of the calendars she'd brought, the book for the year before last. Turning the pages, she made notes on a small pad. When she was finished, she said, 'The year before last, he attended 'C' meetings on February tenth, April thirteenth, June eighth, August tenth, October twelfth, and then December fourteenth. They seem to have been regular enough, all on Tuesdays.' She handed me the list.

'How about the year before that?'

She opened the other book she'd brought, the one for the third year going back, and, turning the pages, read off the dates so I could write them down. 'Regular thing,' she said, when she was done. 'Tuesdays, every other month.'

'You have no idea where he spent those evenings?'

'No.'

'How did he seem, his last day here?'

'For a man whose life was being cut short – a strong, powerful man who had to give up control of an empire he had constructed?' Her lips tightened, then relaxed. 'Actually, he seemed in remarkably good humor that day. He met with several people, dictated a few letters, mostly apologies for matters he could not attend to personally, and left around three o'clock.'

'Did he keep any extra medication in his office?' I asked.

'You mean pills to kill himself?'

'Yes,' I said.

'I went through his office thoroughly. There was no trace of pills.'

I had no doubt she'd searched immediately, looking to destroy any evidence Whitman had taken a deliberate overdose.

'You wouldn't tell me if there were,' I said.

'I find it difficult to believe he killed himself. In any event, there was no trace of an extra supply in his office.'

I believed her like I believed Mrs Johnso⸱ Whitman had no extra pills.

And that was enough for Wendell Phelps to call the cops.

I called his private cell phone number as soon as I got outside. 'I've got something for you to take to the police. Jim Whitman loved his grandsons, and would have known his suicide would null the insurance policy he'd left for their well-being.'

Wendell said nothing for a moment, and then asked, in a surprisingly weak voice, 'Insurance?'

'He had a two-million-dollar life policy, benefitting his grandsons. Death by suicide nulled it.'

Again he paused. 'Perhaps there were other policies . . .' He let the question trail away.

'If there were, his daughter, Debbie, does not know of them. She got nothing for the care of her kids. You have enough to go to the police, Wendell.'

'The cops will say he was a sick man. Pain doesn't make for high lucidity.'

'He was lucid enough to arrange his other bequests.'

'That proves nothing,' he said, his voice stronger, almost combative.

'Then try this: I can't find the source of the pills he supposedly took. He had plenty at home, but he didn't touch those. If he took his own life, he used pills from a secret stash.'

'Cops will say a secret stash was easy to create.'

'He could have been fed those pills. Murdered, as you suspect.'

'Jim Whitman was dying, damn it. There was motive for murder. Cops will laugh.'

'Why fight me on this, Wendell? You suspected right away your friends were being murdered.'

'I overreacted.'

'The night Whitman died, he went downtown to a place that begins with a "C." He went there every two months, always on a Tuesday. He was secretive about it. He had his driver drop him nearby, but never directly at the destination.'

He chuckled, but it sounded forced. 'Whitman was a widower. Maybe he went down there to visit a lady friend he didn't want anyone to know about. Hell, she could have been a high-priced hooker.'

'His regular driver didn't come back for him the night he died. Someone else drove him home, somebody in a light-colored Buick.'

'This is all you've got?' He exhaled disgust into the phone. 'There are thousands of Buicks in this town, like there are thousands of places that begin with the letter "C." I'll get back to you if I want you to continue.'

'Go to the cops,' I said, but I was talking to dead air. He'd hung up.

Wendell had become too argumentative. He'd swatted away every red flag I'd waved. For a man who'd been so certain his fellow tycoons were being murdered, a man who'd been frightened enough to stand by his curtains to make sure they didn't open even an inch, his behavior had transformed suddenly from fear to aggressiveness.

The day was breezy and sunny and good for a walk to mull my new confusion. I headed over

85

to Michigan Avenue, where Jim Whitman had spent the last evening of his life.

Measured by glitz and geography, North Michigan Avenue is the middle sparkler in a three-diamond necklace, approximately equidistant from Rodeo Drive in California and Fifth Avenue in New York. Amanda and I used to walk the grand boulevard when we were new to each other. I was charmed by the way she'd look through the store windows for customers who'd mastered a certain curve to their backs and the oh-so-slight rise to their eyebrows that feigned unconcern to the ridiculous prices of the baubles they were inspecting. 'Arch,' the beautiful girl who'd grown up so rich used to call such false posturing. On North Michigan Avenue, Amanda said, life started and ended with false attitude.

I'd brought Wendell validation of his worries, at least about Jim Whitman. He should have pressed me to find out more. Instead he'd dusted me off with impatience and anger. And arch.

I got to Walton Street, where Whitman had been let off. It was one of the grandest intersections in the city, anchored on the northeast by the Drake Hotel. Upscale shops fanned out from the other three corners, lots of vogue for lots of arch. In the distance, past Lake Shore Drive, Lake Michigan rippled blue and calm, already dotted with the first of the season's sailboats.

I stepped close to the curb to see better in all four directions. I wasn't expecting anything obvious like a neon sign flashing a big orange 'C' or a raven-haired dame in a black dress slit to her hip, blowing C-shaped smoke rings from an upper-story window. I would have settled for even the tiniest of mental nudges, but I didn't even get that. All I saw were sun-washed store-fronts and restaurants offering subtlety at non-subtle prices, and not one had a name that began with a 'C.'

I turned right, walked east on East Walton Place, toward the lake, then reversed, and came west all the way to State Street. I passed the Drake, shiny new storefronts and old three-story graystones – some housing fashionable boutiques and trendy bars, others housing those who hung out in the fashionable boutiques and trendy bars. It was a rich, hip, ever-evolving neighborhood, but mostly it was young, and a seemingly unlikely place for Jim Whitman to visit six times a year. I got back to the Jeep no smarter than when I'd left it and considerably less employed.

I drove south toward the expressway. Michigan Avenue across the bridge is a different place. Gone is the sunny glitz of the boulevard to the north. Michigan Avenue south of the river is dark. The buildings lining its west side are tall and close to the street and shut out the sun from the sidewalk early as it heads away from the lake. There are no strolling swells swinging little boutique bags south of the river, just art students and secretaries, store clerks and podiatrists; people hustling with their heads down just to stay even. And there are pigeons, often dozens of them, strutting and worse on the sidewalk. There is no pretense on Michigan Avenue, south of the river. There is no arch.

But there is often chaos. Unfamiliar drivers heading southbound are often made crazy trying to find the expressway; the signs pointing the way are small and placed too far down. Only at the last moment do the uninitiated comprehend that a left turn is needed to make the right-hand curve to the expressway. And then they swerve, panicked, across several lanes of traffic.

That's what happened that afternoon. The driver in front of me shot across my bow, barely missing my front bumper.

I didn't hit the horn; I didn't raise a fist or a finger. I didn't even remind myself to stay mellow, that this was normal road life Michigan Avenue, south of the river.

I did none of those things because the sight of the car veering in front of me seemed to demand more than that, like I was supposed to focus on what I'd just seen. It was an ordinary enough car – light-colored, beige or tan, swerving in the same stupid way that I'd seen a hundred times before. Yet somehow this car, at this time, seemed very much to matter.

I replayed the image over and over in my mind as I drove back to Rivertown, but I could make no sense of why the image nagged.

Just like I couldn't make sense of Wendell's arch behavior.

Eighteen

I'd just stepped into the turret when a slow ripping creak sounded loud from upstairs. I ran up the wrought iron, knowing, and shot into the kitchen to see for sure.

The turret's craggy, curved limestone walls make for interesting architecture, but they play hell with converting the place into a residence. Hanging anything onto them is a true nightmare. One of the kitchen cabinets I'd just hung was coming loose. I'd arrived home just in time to pull it safely from the wall before it crashed to the floor.

I changed into my rehabbing clothes, which look only marginally worse than my dress duds, and spent the next few hours re-anchoring the cabinet to the wall. By the time I got it to hang right, it was well past dusk, and Amanda had called three times. I'd dodged each call, knowing she must have spoken with her father, and now she wanted truths from me. I didn't want to worry her by saying I suspected Jim Whitman had likely been murdered, and that Wendell didn't want me to learn any more about it.

I walked across what one day might be a hall, and sat at the card table I use as a desk. My cheesy, giveaway black vinyl calendar was nothing like Jim Whitman's leather-bound des* diaries. Though mine was dressed up in g

89

like Whitman's, instead of monogrammed initials, mine sported an air-freight company's logo of an emaciated bird. And where his provided an entire lined page for each day, mine offered a stingy small page for an entire month – space enough, the air freight company must have concluded, for people who don't have much going on in their lives. Certainly they'd been right about me. Save for the leaf counts of the ash by the river, and the few hours I'd invoiced so far that spring, my pages were mostly empty.

I switched on my computer, typed in my bill-able hours for Wendell's final invoice, wrote a check to refund the balance on his retainer, and printed out two copies of the invoice. One went with the check into an envelope addressed to Wendell. The other was for me. Opening the case folder, I saw again the photocopy of Benno Barberi's obituary.

This time, though, the date of his death the previous autumn danced on the paper like it was lit by a strobe: October 11.

I grabbed the notes I'd made just that day. Jim Whitman had scrawled a 'C' in his calendar across the same Tuesday evening Benno Barberi had come home, furious, to die.

I spilled the rest of the file onto the card table, pawing for the newspaper article about Grant Carson's hit-and-run. My hands shook as I read it. He'd been killed on February 15th. It had been a Wednesday, but very early in the morning.

My cell phone rang again. I glanced over. It as Amanda. I let it ring.

I read all the obituaries again, double-checking the dates with my vinyl calendar to be sure. There was no doubt. Benno Barberi, Jim Whitman and Grant Carson had all died on, or just an hour or two following, the second Tuesday of an even-numbered month.

I got out of the chair and went up the stairs to the third floor. I wanted a sweatshirt.

Suddenly, I was cold.

Nineteen

I called Anne Barberi at eight-thirty sharp the next morning.

'No, I can't remember where Benno went that evening,' she said. 'He attended so many dinners.'

'Who has your husband's appointments calendar?'

'His secretary, I would imagine.'

'Can you arrange for me to look at his appointment books for last year and the year before?'

'What have you learned, Mr Elstrom?'

'I'm casting a wide net, trying to gather as much information as I can.'

'What do you suspect?'

'I'll tell you when what I suspect becomes what I believe. For now, tell me, was your husband taking much medication?'

'Of course; several prescriptions. You're wondering why they were ineffective, that last night?'

I was wondering if they'd been too effective, for a killer, but I couldn't dare say that yet. 'Sort of,' l said instead. 'Can you arrange for me to talk to his primary physician?'

'As part of that mysterious wide-net business?'

'Yes.'

'Benno's doctor is a close friend. I'll have him call you.'

And he did, fifteen minutes later. 'What's this about, Elstrom?'

'Was Benno Barberi taking any medication that, in larger than prescribed doses, could have killed him?'

The doctor paused, as he must have often, in this modern era of high-buck medical malpractice suits. And then he evaded. 'Aspirin, taken in large doses, can kill you.'

'Could Barberi have overdosed?'

'The cause of his death was obvious to the EMTs: massive heart attack.'

'He wasn't autopsied?'

'No need.'

'If there were sufficient grounds, can he be autopsied now?'

'Elstrom, you're inferring something untoward? The EMTs would have noticed anything suspicious about Benno's death, as would the emergency room personnel who pronounced him dead.'

'Maybe they didn't probe because his heart condition was well documented.'

'My God, man; you're insinuating he was deliberately overdosed?'

92

'For now, it's something to rule out.'

'Who would benefit from his death? I don't believe Benno had any enemies.'

There was no answering that yet, just as there seemed to be no reason to overdose Jim Whitman, a dying man.

'I need your support to exhume Benno Barberi,' I said.

'Summon divine intervention instead. Benno was cremated and his ashes were scattered off his boat in Lake Michigan.'

Benno Barberi's former secretary called twenty minutes after the doctor slammed down his phone. She was as crisp and as efficient as she'd been the first time we'd spoken. She told me I could come anytime. I left immediately.

She was waiting in the lobby. She was an austere but attractive brunette in her late thirties. If she'd been briefed by Barberi's two sharply barbered assistants about my first visit, she didn't show it. Certainly she did not glance down to see if any varnish or mustard remained on my blazer sleeve.

We went to the same small conference room where I'd met Jason and Brad. Two red leather appointment books sat on the small table.

'I recorded all of Mr Barberi's appointments,' she said. 'What are you looking for?'

'Symmetry,' I said.

'I'm afraid I don't understand,' she said, 'but that's not necessary. Where shall we start?'

'The day and evening of his fatal heart attack.'

She opened one of the books and started turning

pages. 'That would be October eleventh,' she said, stopping at the page. She turned the book around so I could see.

The page was crammed with entries, beginning at seven-thirty in the morning and ending with a notation at five-thirty that read: 'Emerson.' Nothing was posted for the evening.

'What's Emerson?' I asked.

'Emerson is a fitness trainer. Three times a week, Mr Barberi took light exercise, as prescribed by his physician.'

I pulled out my note pad. 'Where's the health club?' I asked.

She smiled. 'In the basement here. Mr Emerson is on staff for our senior executives.'

'Of course,' I said, like I had the lifestyle that would have presumed that. I pointed to the bottom of the calendar page. 'There's nothing written for the evening, yet his wife told me he'd gone out to dinner.'

'I wondered about that.' She looked down at the book. 'He didn't tell me of a dinner engagement, and that was a rarity. His evenings were as busy as his days, and he expected me to keep track of his after-hours obligations as well.'

I started turning the pages backwards. She was right; every one of his evenings, Monday through Saturday, had a notation penned in her handwriting. I didn't find a blank, working-day evening until I'd gone back to August 9.

It, too, had been the second Tuesday of the month.

I turned the book to show her. 'Nothing here, either.'

94

'I guess he forgot to tell me his plans then, as well.'

I continued backwards through the book quickly, growing more certain. And all were there. Or rather, they were not: The evenings of the second Tuesdays in June, April and February had been left blank. I picked up the calendar for the preceding year. It was the same. Benno Barberi had listed no evening appointments for any second Tuesday in February, April, June, August, October or December for two years.

Second Tuesdays, even-numbered months. I closed the second calendar and stood up.

'Did you find what you were looking for?'

'I don't—'

'I know: you don't know.' Her smile was tight and telling. She knew I'd spotted something.

I could only smile back. She walked me downstairs to the fitness center in the basement. Rudy Emerson, dressed in gray sweats, could have been forty or sixty, and looked like he'd never gotten outside a Twinkie in his life.

He remembered his last session with Benno Barberi. 'Of course I knew about his heart. Like always, there was no unusual exertion that day. I started him with easy stretching exercises, we moved to the light weights, and finished with more stretching. Thirty minutes, easy does it. He left here feeling good, looking good.'

'Looking good?' I asked.

'Same suit, but a fresh shirt and a different tie.'

'He sounded good, too? No disorientation, no signs of physical distress?'

95

'Whatever he ate that night might have killed him, but I guarantee it wasn't the exercise he got here.'

'He didn't happen to mention where he was headed?'

Rudy Emerson shook his head. 'Not for a heart attack, that's for sure.'

Barberi's secretary left me in the lobby. Walking out, I had the thought to turn around and look back. Like the last time I'd left Barberi Holdings, I caught sight of a young man in a dark suit watching me. It could have been Brad; it could have been Jason; it could have been someone else, similarly barbered. Whoever he was, he must have caught sight of me looking back, because he quickly moved from sight.

The Rivertown chip pressed down a little on my shoulder, suggesting a little show. I took a leisurely stroll down the rows of the cars parked in the lot.

There were six of the junior-grade black BMWs, each identical to the one that had tailed me at least twice.

A tailing car need not be driven by a killer, I told myself.

Nor did it need be driven by an innocent, either.

I spent a showy moment in front of each car's license plate, writing its number in the little spiral notebook I always carry. Then, back in the Jeep, I checked my cell phone before I started the car, wanting whoever might still be watching to think was running the plate numbers I'd just written wn. And maybe later I'd get a cop friend to do just that. For now, I had other things to think about.

Amanda had left fresh, furious messages, demanding to know why I had not returned any of her calls. Leo offered to buy lunch. And the Bohemian had asked me to call right away. I thumbed his number.

There was no booming 'Vlodek' to begin the conversation, but there was a chuckle, of sorts. 'Arthur Lamm is still missing,' he said.

'You don't sound worried.'

'Perhaps because his absence has become even more explainable. The IRS began investigating him last fall.'

'For what?'

'Unreported income from insurance irregularities.'

'Insurance? I thought the guy was in real estate.'

'Arthur might have the longest tentacles of those in the heavy cream. He acts as a broker, selling large office buildings. Then he negotiates to become its property manager. To top it all off, he gets the property owner to buy the building's insurance from his agency.'

'An IRS investigation wouldn't make a guy like Lamm run into the woods,' I said.

'Of course, unless his battery of high-priced attorneys told him to get lost until they could work something out with the Feds.'

'Or unless he committed big-time fraud?' I asked. 'Such things can attract long pris sentences. In which case, he wouldn't run off the woods of Wisconsin. He'd flee the co go someplace where he can't be extradite

'Look, we already know his rowboat and fishing gear are all gone, and that his cottage is on a string of lakes,' the Bohemian said. 'I suppose we could see something clandestine in that. I guess it's possible he could have headed north to Canada, and from there gone overseas.'

'Or he's staged things, leaving a false trail to buy time to leave the country another way.'

'This might be of interest to some of his associates,' the Bohemian said. 'Those in the heavy cream often cross-invest in each other's companies.'

'You want me to look more deeply into it?'

'I want you to be ready.'

Twenty

Rikk, at Carson's life insurance carrier, sounded half asleep when he picked up the phone.

'Did anybody identify where Carson went, his last night?' I asked.

He yawned, quite audibly. 'You're killing me, Elstrom. You already asked that. Our concern starts at the moment he got smacked. Dinner doesn't matter.'

'Didn't your investigator ask, anyway?'

'Maybe; probably; I don't know. How does knowing where he ate help us?'

'You never know,' I invented. 'Maybe he was something that disoriented him, made him out in front of traffic.'

d we could sue the restaurant or his dinner

98

companions to recover our payout? You think he was murdered? For what purpose?'

'I don't know,' I said.

'You're reaching.' He yawned, and added, 'As well as holding back.'

'I'm wondering if someone was with Carson, in the car.' I said, thinking specifically of the man in the tan Buick who drove Whitman home.

'Listen, Elstrom, asking these questions helps us only if the passenger was wealthy, had a hand in forcing Carson in front of the kill car, and we could sue to recover. We discussed all this. Vehicular homicides are too chancy. There are better ways to kill.'

'That's what any right-thinking person would think. That's what makes it a clever way to murder.'

'Give me a motive.'

'I don't have one.'

'There were no witnesses, remember? Even if you found a motive, we can't prove anything.'

'At least find out where Carson went, before he got killed.'

'If I call our investigator, will you leave me alone?'

'If you will also check Grant Carson's appointment books for the last two years, to see if he went to that same place on the second Tuesday evenings of every even-numbered month.'

That woke him up. 'What the hell do you know that you're not telling me?' he shouted.

'Help me here, Rikk.'

'How can I rationalize asking for calendars?'

'With creativity.'

'You're nuts, Elstrom,' he said, and hung up.

I called Leo after I'd gotten on the tollway, southbound. 'You said you're buying lunch?'

'Yes, but I'm dieting.'

Leo's metabolism runs as fast as his intellect. There'd been no change in his 140 pounds since high school. 'You're porking up?' I asked anyway.

'A pound and a half since Christmas.'

'I can achieve that with a lone raspberry Danish.'

'So I noticed on my front stoop, very recently. See you at Kutz's.'

I'd saved the worst call for last. I thumbed on my cell phone directory and clicked Amanda's number. 'Hey, sorry I haven't been returning your calls,' I said. 'I've been swamped . . .'

Her voice was barely audible in the headset I'd bought cheap at the Discount Den. Then again, I was surrounded by trucks.

'I can't hear you,' I yelled, speeding up to get clear of the trucks.

'Do you miss me?' she shouted.

'Like there'll be no tomorrow, Amanda,' I screamed, joking, at last getting free of the trucks.

'Jenny,' the voice yelled, horribly clear. 'Jenny Galecki.'

'Ah,' I said, hearing too perfectly. For sure, jackasses should not be issued speed-dial features, ~ thumbs, or headsets. Or mouths.

Talking with Amanda, are we?' she asked.

's that case involving her father that I told ʾout,' I said, fighting the urge to say I wasn't

100

'Did you get my little package?' There was frost in the words that I couldn't blame on the cheap headset.

'Package? No.'

'I sent you a little something, to keep you thinking of me. It seemed funny at the time.' She clicked off.

In the eight months since Jenny went west, we sometimes went weeks without speaking. Still, an hour didn't pass where I didn't think of her, hoping an hour hadn't passed where she hadn't thought of me. And somehow San Francisco seemed closer.

Now I'd messed things for sure by fumbling my mention of Amanda. San Francisco felt like it had moved to another continent.

The phone rang again as I got off the tollway. 'Listen, Jenny—'

'Damn you, Elstrom,' Gaylord Rikk corrected. It had only been twenty minutes since we'd spoken. I ripped the headset off and pressed the phone to my ear, in clear violation of Illinois law.

'That seems to have already happened.'

'I got intrigued, but only because I'm bored. In some disgusting way, you liven up my dreary existence.'

'You've got something?' I asked.

'It only took two phone calls. Turns out our people did ask where Carson had gone, the night he was killed. No one seemed to know, not his wife or his secretary, and we dropped it because it didn't seem relevant. So . . .' He lingered in silent smugness, waiting.

'So?' I asked, accepting the cue.

He dropped his voice, a secret agent for sure. 'I called Carson's secretary, saying I was tidying up the last of our paperwork, and needed to know where he'd been that night. She said she already told the police she didn't know, which I knew.'

'And?' I asked, anxious. He'd learned something.

'Nothing,' he said.

'You struck out?'

'No, I mean Carson had nothing written on his calendar for that evening.'

'I don't suppose—'

'I caught your drift earlier,' he said. 'I schmoozed. Carson's secretary had his appointment books, five years' worth, right at her desk.'

'And?'

'Nothing was written in for any of those Tuesday evenings.'

'You're sure?'

'Why do you sound so excited?'

'I'll tell you in a minute.'

'His secretary thought it was unusual because he was always busy at night. But she double-checked because I was so persuasive. Nothing had been penciled in for any of those evenings. And that, to her, is inconceivable.'

It was inconceivable to me as well, almost.

'Tell me how this is going to help me sue the beneficiary, Elstrom,' he said.

'Who is the beneficiary?'

'I can't divulge the entity.'

'Entity? The beneficiary wasn't family?'

'I'm sure Carson had multiple policies. We only

102

carried one of them, and the beneficiary wasn't family. It was an organization, a company. Tell me how you're going to help us.'

I told him I'd call him when I learned more, and clicked him away, but not before I heard him swear.

I swore, too, at the bulb flickering stronger in the back of my brain. Grant Carson had been careful to make no notation of where he'd been off to, those Tuesday nights. As had Benno Barberi. Jim Whitman had noted them in his appointment books only with the letter 'C.' Whatever those three men had been doing, they were doing it secretly, and they were doing it together.

Right down to getting killed, one after the other.

Twenty-One

I skidded to a dusty stop across the few stones left on Kutz's gravel lot with what I thought was considerable élan.

Leo was waiting in his Porsche. The top was down, but he'd parked in the shade under the overpass, and he wore an oversized red straw hat that, even without its tightly knotted blue chin-strap, would have looked ridiculous. Thought it was months before the burning rays of summer, Leo was careful; his pale skin burns like infant's.

'So elegant, your driving finesse,' he said

'I know the words to that bit of music you're listening to,' I said, through the newly exposed rip in my side curtain. Another curl of Discount Den duct tape had let go on the tollway.

'They're called lyrics, you boor, but Jobim didn't use them in this song.'

He was listening to a piece of Brazilian bossa nova that, for once, I recognized. I didn't know its name, but it was smooth and flowing and getting a lot of play as background in a television laxative commercial.

'No more pressure,' I began singing, warbling with the same solemnity as the singer on TV.

He sighed, shut off the player, and got out of the car.

We walked up to the peeling wood trailer. Young Kutz glowered at us through the tiny order window. Young Kutz is young in name only; he's on the wrong side of eighty, and had been glowering from his trailer long before Leo and I started coming in grammar school.

'Hiya, Mr Kutz,' Leo said.

'What's it today, twerp?'

Leo stretched up to his full five foot six inches so he could line his eyes along the counter. 'The usual six pups, cheese fries, and Big Swallow root beer, of course.'

'I thought you were dieting,' I said.

'The trick is to chew slowly, thereby atomizing all the fat calories before swallowing.'

'For sure you'll drop that nettlesome pound d a half.' I added my one dog and small diet his order, gave Leo eight singles – Kutz's s were an outrage, given the quality of the

104

food – and went around to the back of the trailer.

The lunch rush was over and empty picnic tables were everywhere. The snow was long gone, and it hadn't rained at all in March, yet incredibly, I found a table that was almost half free of pigeon droppings.

Leo noticed when he came with the food. 'Partially dropless – nice,' he said, setting down the flimsy tray of hotdogs, fries and drinks with a careful, soft sliding motion of his hands and forearms. Kutz uses ultra-thin plastic trays because they're likely to flex and be dropped, resulting in re-orders as well as queasy pigeons, which then results in excessively spotted tables.

As always, we ate silently for the first minutes, savoring the truck exhaust drifting down from the overpass mingling with the steam we imagined might be rising from our barely lukewarm hot dogs. They were the exact smells of our youth, nostalgia at its purest. Rumor had it Kutz had never changed the hot dog water in all the years he worked the trailer. No need, he'd supposedly once said: grease floats and ends up on the product, to be consumed by customers or pigeons – depending. That meant the hot dogs Leo and I were now eating might have been cooked in part of the very water Kutz used when we were kids. Nostalgia doesn't get any purer than that.

'You may now tap the power of my formidab brain,' Leo said, after his third hot dog. 'Ho the case?'

I told him that Barberi, Whitman and ﹰ

had all died on, or right after, the second Tuesdays of even-numbered months.

He slammed the brakes on the sagging cheese fry he was about to propel into his mouth. When I dare eat Kutz's cheese fries, I use a plastic spoon because the yellowish substance he says is cheese quickly dissolves potato fiber, rendering them too limp for me to hold. Not Leo. He regards Kutz's cheese fries as among life's worthiest adversaries, and while still in high school, mastered the art of arcing them into his mouth with his fingers. He says it's a matter of wrist speed and pride.

Now, all that was forgotten. The cheese fry slid from his fingers to drop, with a soft, gelatinous slap, back into its cardboard tray. 'What have you made of that?'

'Each of the three men took pains to obscure their whereabouts those nights.' I told him of the 'C' notations in Whitman's desk diary.

'They were together, at this "C" place,' he said.

'Until they started dying, one by one.'

'What's premeditated and sinister in a heart attack, an understandable suicide and a random hit-and-run?'

'What if the first and second deaths came from administered overdoses, and the hit and run was deliberate? Barberi came home highly agitated over some insurance concern, but he'd learned to handle stress. A dose of something might have nt his heart into overdrive, but we'll never w; he was cremated. We do know Whitman ted too many pills, and right now we know vas no good reason for him to go outside

106

his home to get them. If Whitman was murdered, then it's likely Carson was murdered too, pushed in front of an oncoming car.'

'To what end?'

'I don't know.'

'Does Wendell have any thoughts on motive?'

'He fired me.'

The eyebrows came together and stuck, shocked. 'Surely not for a lack of progress.'

'His whole attitude has changed. Instead of being intrigued by my suspicions, Wendell became combative and swatted every one of them away.'

'What did he say about those mysterious "C" notations in Whitman's calendar?'

'No curiosity there, either.'

'He knows what they mean,' he said.

'He spent those Tuesday evenings with Barberi, Whitman and Carson,' I said, 'and I'll bet he knows who drove Whitman home.'

'You've gotten too close,' Leo said.

'Yes.'

'What's next?' he asked.

'Arthur Lamm.'

Leo shook his head, confused. 'The real-estate biggie?'

'He's gone missing, though it might be because the IRS is investigating him.' I told him what the Bohemian had learned.

'What if he didn't take off?'

'Then twenty-five per cent of the biggest sh in Chicago have just been murdered.'

Twenty-Two

'My father fired you.' Amanda spoke slowly over the phone, each word precise, distinct, and under control. I knew that control. She was furious.

'Apparently.'

'He told me you'd made no progress, you'd pocketed his two-thousand-dollar retainer without doing anything but mewing around a little bit, and dusted him off by telling him to go to the police.'

'Mewing? Like a cat? He said I was mewing?'

'Don't evade. What is he up to?'

'Actually, I've made out a check for his refund.'

'Don't parse my words, either. What's all this about: the bodyguards, the secrecy? Is his life in danger?'

I'd had an inspiration, driving home from Kutz's. 'I want to deliver the refund in person. I'm certain he won't take my call, or see me at his office.'

'You want me to set up a confrontation without telling me what's going on?'

'He's still my client.'

'I ask again: is his life in danger?'

'Get me in front of him, Amanda. If I learn ɘ's in real trouble, I will violate his trust and ᵈ you.'

ʷas enough, for the moment. She said she'd ᵉᵏ to me.

ˢed the second floor, headed to see how

108

my freshly re-hung cabinet was faring, when the lid on the front door mail slot clanked. I'd installed one that was extra-large, anticipating improved times, but even the junk mailers didn't yet think me worthy. Today though, my mail slot clanked. Mail had come. I clanked, too, beating down the wrought-iron stairs.

It was Jenny's small something, sent in a padded envelope. I ripped it open. An untied purple bowtie was inside, with a note that read, 'It's not so much the look that's sought, but rather the demonstration of proficiency.'

It was a nudge, aimed with a joke, and so quintessentially, marvelously Jenny.

I'd never tied a bowtie. That was the laugh, and the nudge, because she knew I'd wrestle with learning to tie the thing, and think of her every second I was doing it. And I would, along with thinking about my aborted trip to San Francisco and the phone call I'd fumbled just a few hours earlier.

I took my bowtie upstairs. The cabinet I'd straightened was listing. Not much, just a few degrees, and surely no more than the smoke stacks on the *Titanic* had tipped in the first minutes following its collision with the iceberg. I set down the tie and spent the next hour trying to correct the cabinet, but no amount of shim-ming, leveling, and shaving got it to hang right.

Amanda called. 'We're having barbecue tonight with my father, at five.'

'That's early,' I said.

'With the pig lady,' she said. It was ro˙ especially for Amanda.

'You mean his wife?'

'Second wife,' she said.

I knew that, of course. It had been in the papers. Wendell, a long-time widower, had married after Amanda and I divorced.

'You'll have time to tell me everything as we drive up there,' she said. 'Everything.'

Amanda was waiting beneath the portico of her lakeside condominium building. She wore exquisitely fitted jeans and a burgundy top that didn't pull all the fire from her eyes. She flashed the rest of it at me as she slid onto the passenger's seat. 'I don't like cagy.'

'For the time being, I have to respect your father's confidence,' I said as I pulled onto Lake Shore Drive.

She gave my invariable khakis and blue shirt the usual quick glance, but lingered at my neck. Her voice softened. 'A bow tie, and purple?'

'Shock and awe.' It had taken me an hour practicing with downloaded instructions to achieve the partially crumpled mess around my neck.

'You want my father to be shocked and awed by your tie, or by what you're going to say?'

I didn't want to say I'd worn the tie to keep reminding myself of who'd sent it, and I didn't want to tell her of the accusations I was going to lay on Wendell, so I said nothing.

She fingered the wires sticking out of the hole ͏n the dashboard where the radio had been. 'You ͏ed to have a Mercedes,' she said.

͏Bought used,' I said.

͏d such very nice clothes.'

110

'Fortunes wane.'

'Perhaps, but you gave your clothes away, right after we split up. Including that nice camel-hair sport coat I bought you for your birthday . . .' Her voice trailed off.

It was old detritus, and it was accurate. And it was useful, because it beat discussing what her father hadn't told me about Barberi, Whitman and Carson.

'I'd gotten to living a little too fancy,' I said. 'Jettisoning the duds and the car seemed a reasonable way to simplify my life.'

'Along with going to live in a turret?'

'You are demeaning my castle?'

'You have to admit, there's something monastic about your life . . . the turret, the lack of variety in clothing, this . . .' She bent back one of the wires sticking out from the dash, and turned to me. 'Was I part of all your clutter, Dek? Was I too fancy?'

'Too fancy?' I repeated, startled. 'You've never been too fancy, Amanda.'

It might have been from the rapid turns in the road, but she'd leaned closer before shifting away. 'Your new bow tie is a promising addition to your wardrobe,' she said. 'What prompted you to buy it?'

'It was a gift . . .' I stopped, though my abrupt silence spilled the rest of it.

'Ah . . . the newswoman.' Then, 'What are you going to ask my father?' she asked, leaning more toward her door and safer talk.

Or more dangerous, depending. 'I'm going to ask him about Wendell Phelps.'

111

She turned to look at me. 'What the hell?'

'I'm going to ask him if he fired his previous investigator using the same baloney he gave me.'

I told her I wanted to talk to Wendell before I said anything more, and we fell into silence as she mulled, and I mulled, things each of us didn't understand about Wendell and perhaps, less than fleetingly, about ourselves. I tried to fill the quiet by shifting more than was necessary, working through the rush-hour traffic up Lake Shore Drive to Sheridan Road, through Evanston, Wilmette, and Winnetka. With every mile, the homes got grander and set back farther from the road. By the time we got to Lake Forest, most of the estates were invisible.

I turned right onto Red Leaf Road and followed it as it curved along the shore of Lake Michigan. As I rounded the last turn, brake lights flashed ahead as cars slowed to turn through Wendell's stone pillars.

Amanda inhaled sharply. 'He didn't tell me he was having a party. I'm wearing jeans, for God's sake.'

'Nice jeans, though,' I said. 'And of course, I'm wearing a purple bow tie.'

She didn't laugh.

We passed a bush that looked like it had been ripped in half.

'Pigs,' she said. Earlier, she'd referred to her father's new wife as a pig lady, but now, apparently, she was including Wendell in her contempt.

I followed a black Mercedes sedan into the long driveway and coasted to a stop. Four more dark Mercedes were ahead of the one in front of

112

us. At the head of the line, several blue-jacketed parking valets were waiting for a uniformed security guard to check invitations. It took ten minutes for the guard to get to us.

Amanda leaned across me and spoke through the rip in my side curtain. 'I'm Amanda Phelps. I've brought a guest.'

I found myself holding my breath. Her body weight, so easily pressed against me, felt like the best of our old times.

The private cop's list of invited guests had small photos alongside the names. He peered in at her. 'I'm sorry, Ms Phelps, we don't have your guest listed.'

'I'm Mr Phelps's daughter. That's sufficient.'

The private cop looked a little too long at the gray primed section behind the driver's side door before asking for my driver's license. Amanda had to straighten up so I could reach for my wallet. I handed out my license, and the guard stepped back to speak into his two-way radio.

'Obviously I didn't tell my father you'd be coming along,' she said to me.

I gestured toward the guard reporting my arrival. 'There goes my shock and awe.'

'Maybe not. My father hasn't yet seen your purple bow tie.'

Behind us, expensive automobile engines revved loud and impatient. Finally, the radio crackled and the guard motioned for one of the valets to come over. 'Thank you,' the private cop said, handing back my license.

'Don't let anybody paint over that primer,' I told the valet as I got out, pointing at the gray

113

patch behind the driver's door. He nodded gravely, probably thinking it was a sign of great wealth to have the confidence to drive up in such a heap, particularly wearing a purple bow tie.

A big man was waiting for us by the front walk, his suit coat bulging from a gun. He motioned for Amanda and me to follow him along the flagstone path around the south side of the house. Wendell had sent him out fast when he learned Amanda had brought a most unwanted guest.

A huge red-and-white striped tent had been set up on the lawn. A four-piece combo was playing gentle jazz on the stone terrace as a hundred people, holding champagne flutes, swayed to the music and made appropriate rich people noises. The unseasonably warm weather had held, and the men wore pastel jackets, the women, pastel dresses. All the guests seemed to be tanned, from Palm Beach or Palm Springs or wherever the palms were where they wintered when Chicago got slushy. I supposed I stood out, because I don't get tanned until summer, and even then it comes mottled with spots of white wherever bits of caulk and paint had blocked the sun from my skin.

I looked around for Wendell. Three more men in ill-fitting, too-square suits stood fairly close together at one end of the terrace. Wendell stood in the approximate middle of them, talking with a small group of people. I started to head over but the big man blocked my way. 'Mr Phelps is busy.'

'Not for his daughter,' Amanda said.

'Mr Phelps suggested later,' the big man said. Wendell had allowed me in, only to box me in.

Amanda was about to head for her father when a bell sounded from a few hundred feet away. The jazz group stopped playing in mid-riff.

'Delores's new baby,' a woman with impossibly white teeth said to Amanda. Delores was the name of Wendell's second wife.

The crowd began to move as a herd toward the far side of the lawn. I looked toward the tent. Wendell had gone.

I grabbed two flutes of champagne from a passing waiter. 'Delores's new baby?' I whispered to Amanda, handing her one. 'You've become a half-sister?'

I'd expected a glare. Instead, Amanda gave me a faint smile and we followed the crowd.

Twenty-Three

Only the waves crashing onto the beach below sounded as we moved, hushed like congregants summoned to a secret sunset ceremony, through a tall grass prairie preserve and into a dense tunnel of arched trees that shrouded the path in almost complete darkness. We emerged fifty yards later into a clearing where the last of the day's sun shone again. Some of those ahead of us had apparently participated in such gatherings before, and were forming a broad semicircle facing a lit-up, miniature stone cottage.

A large woman stood in front of the tiny house. Her closely cropped dark hair was str with gray, and she wore a loose-flowing, multi-hued robe that, in the backlighting from the little windows behind her, made her look like a pagan priestess afire with the setting sun. She held a champagne flute in her right hand, and the end of a leash in the other. I stepped around the people in front to see more clearly. The other end of the leash was attached to a pig.

It was not the sort of small pink pig seen on farms, destined to become bacon. This pig was larger, with brown and white spots, and looked to weigh two hundred pounds.

The woman in the robe raised her champagne. 'Welcome Jasmine, everybody,' she shouted to the sky.

Everyone raised their glasses.

As I raised my champagne, I snuck a glance at Amanda. She was looking directly back at me, her own flute raised, but not toward the pig. She was toasting my ignorance. 'My new half-sister,' she mouthed above the muffled applause, the best the crowd could do while holding champagne.

After a few last claps, and several more shouts of 'Welcome, Jasmine,' the group began to disperse in the direction of the path back to the food and stronger booze. The homage had ended. I turned to follow, when Amanda stepped up and seized my hand.

'No, Vlodek,' she said. It was the first time she'd ever used my given name. 'You must meet Delores, the woman at the center of my father's t-quite-rational universe.'

er fingernails dug into my palm as she half d me to the small group of people clustered around the woman in robes. As we got closer to the cottage, I noticed that the thick Plexiglas windows were deeply scratched and smeared milky, no doubt from snouts.

Just then, the rubber door swung outward and, to the faint strains of classical music playing inside, another pig lumbered out, this one pure black and half the size of the leashed Jasmine. I glimpsed straw on the floor of the rock cottage before the rubber door slapped shut.

Delores spotted Amanda standing at the edge of the little group. The way the two women stiffened simultaneously said it all. Amanda put her arm under my elbow and marched me forward.

'Amanda,' Delores Phelps said.

'Delores.'

People to the left of us stepped back, to make room for the pig that had come from the cottage.

'Peter!' Delores Phelps cried, holding out her champagne flute low enough for the new arrival, the black pig, to insert his tongue. 'Peter just loves Dom Perignon,' Delores said.

Several in the small cluster murmured approvingly, and Peter the pig grunted, a low, long snorting sound, likely in agreement.

Delores turned to me. 'And you are Mr Rudolph, Amanda's most successful young man?'

'Not young, nor successful, nor Mr Rudolph. I'm Dek Elstrom.'

'We're divorced,' Amanda said, of me.

'I believe I did hear something about that,' Delores said. 'Lovely tie, Mr Elstrom.'

Peter nudged Delores for more Dom Perigno

'Peter is so attached to his mommy, aren't y

117

Peter?' Delores cooed, lowering her flute to give him another taste. 'Peter is a Vietnamese pot-bellied pig,' she said. 'He used to sleep in his own bedroom, just down the hall from ours, but after he outgrew his bassinet, he started coming into our bedroom.' She stopped, noticing the look on my face. 'He was mostly potty trained, of course, but still, he did have his accidents.' She bent down again to nuzzle the pig's hairy ear. 'So we built him his own little cottage, and got him some brothers and sisters.' She straightened up and nodded to the pig at the other end of the leash. 'Jasmine's our newest, a Kunekune from New Zealand.'

I looked at my empty champagne flute, simply because I couldn't think of what to say.

Delores noticed, and held out her own flute, swishing the little in the bottom that Peter had not licked out.

I shook my head. 'Thank you, no.' I took a quick look around for Amanda, but she'd disappeared. Only the bodyguard remained.

'It was lovely meeting you,' I told Delores Phelps.

'Likewise, I'm sure.'

'You, too,' I said to the guard, but he made no move to step away. We walked back to the mansion, me in front, him a close two steps behind.

Amanda was talking to her father on the terrace. 'What have you been telling my daughter, Elstrom?' he asked, when I walked up.

'That you've not been forthcoming, and nothing ᵉ.'

118

'We'll discuss your ignorance privately.' Then, to Amanda, 'Just he and I, my dear.'

'I'm part of this,' she said.

'I'll explain later,' he said.

For a moment he stood silent, I stood silent, and she glared. Finally, she shrugged and walked away.

Wendell led us across the lawn, a small parade with him in the lead, me in the middle, and three body guards bringing up the rear. We entered the house through a side door and passed a laundry room with a porcelain-topped table for folding clothes and a kitchen fitted out, wall-to-wall, with stainless steel. A right turn down another hall brought us to the passage that led to his study door. We didn't go in. The three guards moved up close behind me as Wendell continued marching us through the long dark foyer to the front of the house.

'What are you hiding, Wendell?' I asked the back of his head.

He opened the front door. 'Why call the police?'

'I didn't call any cops.'

He stepped back, and two of the three guards came up on either side of me. I took the hint. I pressed Wendell's refund check onto the guard at my right, and stepped outside. The door slammed.

A valet had been alerted to bring up the Jee I got in and drove through the gates. I pu over fifty yards from the house and Amanda. Her phone went automatically mail. I didn't leave a message because noticed the glint of a familiar bumpe past a copse of trees alongside the road ahead. I started up, motored past without looking directly at the driver. It didn't take long to be sure. The car, a black junior-grade BMW, pulled out and stayed far back at every turn, from Lake Forest all the way south and into Evanston.

I found the sort of cul-de-sac I was looking for just before I got to the outskirts of Chicago. I turned in, spun around fast, and was waiting for him when he eased into the cul-de-sac. He slammed on his brakes but he was too late; I'd pulled sideways to block him in. I jumped out of my car.

His window was open, and so was his collar. I reached in and grabbed it.

It was Jason, or Brad. I couldn't tell because they'd been so similarly barbered.

'Tell Mrs Barberi that I'll report when I'm ready,' I shouted. 'And tell yourself that if I see you again, I'll break your snout.'

As I got back into the Jeep and drove away, I realized I'd misspoken. I'd meant to say nose, not snout.

It had been that sort of day.

Twenty-Four

fellow flashing a badge early the next after-
d to be one of the cops Wendell accused
ling. He didn't look like a cop. Blond
faced, he wore a gray herringbone

sport coat, charcoal slacks, a white shirt and a blue-striped tie. Right down to his highly polished burgundy penny loafers, he looked bound for the Ivy League, Princeton perhaps. He said his name was Delmar. I asked if that was a first name or a last name. He said his first name was Delray.

'Delray Delmar?'

'I figured a guy named Vlodek would understand.'

'Like we were joined at the hip.' I invited him in.

'Nifty,' he said, looking around the bare limestone room. First-time visitors are always impressed with the craggy, curved limestone walls and the beamed wood ceiling, though typically they offer up more than one word of architectural praise.

I motioned for us to sit in the two white plastic chairs. Except for those, two cans of varnish and my table saw, the first floor is unfurnished.

'I know how it is, starting out,' he said.

I was old enough to be his father, almost. Mature enough, certainly, to control my temper.

'I'm saving up for furniture, too,' he added after another beat, as if that helped.

I fought the urge to ask if he'd like some chocolate milk. He might have said yes, and I didn't have any. Milk. Or chocolate. So I stayed silent and stared at the knot of his striped tie.

He cleared his throat. 'You were hired by Wendell Phelps to investigate the recent d of three prominent businessmen?'

He was asking two troublesome ques'

121

wanted me to confirm the identity of a client, something I wouldn't do. And he was asking me to admit to running an investigation, terminology I had to tiptoe around, because 'investigate' is a touchy verb in official Illinois. Investigators – private detectives – are required to be licensed, and that in turn requires law enforcement experience or a law degree. I had neither. But there's a loophole, as there usually is in Illinois laws: a person can operate as an investigator if he's working for a lawyer. It's a gray line, but it's a mile wide. I knew several lawyers, including the Bohemian, who would cover for me if I ever got in trouble. Still, I like to dodge the word 'investigate.'

'Did Wendell Phelps tell you that?' I said, instead of answering.

'I got your name from Debbie Goring, who was delighted to talk to me. It didn't take much Internet research to learn that you nibble at investigating. I also learned you are Mr Phelps's son-in-law.'

'Former son-in-law,' I said.

'Mr Phelps is a friend to many powerful people, including Arthur Lamm,' he said, floating the name while watching my eyes.

The kid had a contact in the IRS. 'I went to see Mr Phelps,' he went on. 'One of his guards said he wasn't home. So now I've come to see you.'

'I'm a records researcher,' I told the lad. 'tly I work for insurance companies, though down information for law firms as well.'

'or Wendell Phelps?'

'I agree with Debbie Goring. I'm troubled by where Jim Whitman got the pills to kill himself.'

'I believe you're also bothered by the timing of the deaths of Benno Barberi and Grant Carson because they, like Jim Whitman, died on or just after the second Tuesdays of even-numbered months.' Young Delray Delmar had also talked to Barberi's and Carson's secretaries.

'Therefore,' he went on, 'you've probably deduced that the three dead men spent those Tuesday evenings together.'

I liked the way he applied the word 'deduced' to my thinking. It made me sound like something other than a schlump who couldn't hang a kitchen cabinet straight.

'By Jove, Holmes, it's an interesting puzzle,' I said.

'Work with me, Mr Elstrom. I'm not interested in Wendell Phelps. You can continue to protect Mr Phelps and perhaps help Debbie Goring. She might even part with some large dollars if you help her gain insurance money.'

'Who are you really interested in?'

He leaned forward. 'Arthur Lamm. What do you know about him?'

'If he's not gone fishing, then he's gone missing,' I said, rhythmically.

'I think he's on the run,' he said.

'From the IRS?' I asked.

'Surely from them, but I'm wondering if he running from something more. I want to quest him about those deaths. Do you know whe might be?'

123

'No. Do you think he killed Whitman and Carson?'

'All I think right now is he travels in the same circles as the dead men and now he's disappeared.'

'Do you think he's part of that Tuesday evening group?' I asked.

'He's wealthy enough. Do you have any idea where they hold their get-togethers?'

'No idea.' It was true enough. All I had was the letter 'C,' and I wasn't going to share that without Wendell's permission.

'Somewhere north of the Chicago River, on the Gold Coast?' he asked.

'Because that's where Grant Carson was killed?' I shook my head. 'Are you in Homicide?'

'Special Projects.'

'I've never heard of it. How many are in that department?'

'Just me.'

'Why isn't Homicide looking into this?'

'Not enough heat yet.' Delray grinned. 'My boss respects unofficial inquiries from powerful men.'

'Someone asked your boss to look into Arthur Lamm?'

'You got it.' He stood up. 'I'm going to take apart Grant Carson's hit-and-run, because it's the freshest death. I'm looking at Whitman, too, because his daughter, and you, can't figure where ⁀e got those extra pills or even why he would ⁄e bothered. I'm saving Benno Barberi for last, ⁀use frankly, I see nothing in his death that sts murder.'

'And Arthur Lamm?'

'I'm interested in him most of all.' We walked outside. 'Keep me informed, and I'll do likewise. I'll even put in good words to Debbie Goring, help you get a reward. But we do things my way.'

'Who's your rabbi?' In Chicago-speak, a rabbi is a clout guy, somebody connected, a person who can take care of getting whatever a kid in a striped tie needed.

Grinning, he said, 'The deputy chief,' and got into his car.

As I watched him drive away in his long black cop sedan, I saw a young, brash, arrogant guy who knew how to get clouted into a job. He was ambitious, and he had power behind him. He'd be relentless; he'd learn things.

Some of which would lead him straight to Wendell Phelps and whatever he was hiding.

Twenty-Five

The cell number Wendell had given me no longer worked. It must have been a disposable, discarded like me.

I mulled, but not for long. I owed Amanda an explanation for last night, and a warning abo the cop who was likely to complicate her fath life.

I called her cell phone six times in thre and left no messages. She answered the angrily.

'You dumped me,' she said.

'Your father had me thrown out.'

'He said you stormed off.'

'He accused me of calling the cops. One was just here.'

'Why would you call the cops?'

'I didn't. You know I'd never rat out a client . . .' I paused, a hypocrite, about to do just that. 'It must have been someone else in the heavy cream who called—'

'*The heavy cream?*' she interrupted, almost shouting with impatience.

'They're the people who have risen to the very top, people like your father, who run Chicago. One of them must have gotten scared and called the Chicago police. Delray Delmar, a pup but earnest, caught the case, and came round to ask what I knew.'

'Scared by what?'

'Your father told you nothing last night?'

'Only that you blew up and left. I tried to press him. He mumbled something about talking later and walked away. For the next hour, he kept himself surrounded by others. Obviously he was avoiding me, so I got one of the guards to drive me home.' She paused for a moment, then said, 'You could have waited out on the street, you know.'

'I called you from outside, but your phone was ⸱tched off. Then I realized I'd been followed. ⸱s safest to leave you with your father's ⸱'

⸱ scaring me. Who was following you?'

⸱Barberi's widow put a tail on me. She

126

knows I'm chasing the case and doesn't want to wait for information. I put a stop to it.'

'Is Mrs Barberi frightened like my father? Benno died last year from a heart attack.'

'Did you know Jim Whitman, or Grant Carson?'

'Benno Barberi died of a heart attack, right?'

'All signs point to that.'

'And Mr Whitman and Mr Carson . . .?' She stopped, understanding. 'This is why my father hired bodyguards? He sees something sinister in their deaths?'

'Yes.'

'But Mr Whitman technically died of natural causes, though he may have swallowed too many pain killers. Mr Carson was hit by a car.'

'There are wrinkles surrounding each death.'

'I ask now for the third time: is my father in danger?'

'He'll be in less danger if he tells the cops what he knows. Do you know Arthur Lamm?'

'Don't change the subject.'

'I'm not.'

'Arthur is my father's closest friend,' she said. 'He handles our corporate insurance, and my father has invested in a couple of Arthur's real-estate ventures. Is Arthur in danger, too?'

'He's dropped from sight. He might have gone camping, or he might be evading the IRS.'

'I heard a rumor about the IRS investigation. but Arthur wouldn't run from that. He's g lawyers and accountants to take care of s things. If he's not around, it's because he's camping . . . Right, Dek?'

'I'd like to be sure he's gone camping

127

'You believe my father's not delusional, that someone's out to kill the men in the . . . whatever.'

'Heavy cream,' I said, supplying the words. 'Wendell won't tell me what he knows. Young officer Delmar has better resources than mine, and he'll find out what that is.'

'This can't be real,' she said, but she said she'd talk to her father.

On the stoop, outside his bungalow, Leo went straight for a vein. 'You, pass for a rich guy?' He laughed.

'Just for a night, maybe two. I'll breeze up to Lamm's fishing camp and see if I can sniff out his whereabouts.'

'Because you think that's something Lamm's friends, family, Wendell's previous investigator, the IRS, and most especially your new young cop friend haven't been sharp enough to consider doing themselves?'

'Because I don't know what to think.'

'Your cop is OK with you pursuing this on your own?'

'I promised I'd report anything I find out.'

'Meaning you'll report anything that doesn't incriminate Wendell.'

'I'm sure he understands.'

A sly grin lit Leo's face. 'Merely driving my car won't pass you as rich enough to be a friend Lamm's,' he said. 'You've got to have the ds, too.' He touched the hem of his tropical like he was caressing imperial silk. 'Red and yellow flowers on blue rayon are the true signs of affluence. They make you look wealthy enough to not give a damn.'

'I want to look like I own the Porsche, not like I stole it.'

He sighed and handed over the keys.

Twenty-Six

Two hours north of Milwaukee, the concrete highway softened into rippling blacktop and the barns began fading from freshly painted reds to chalking shades of rose. An hour north of that, the blacktop crumbled and so had some of the barns. Every few miles, I spotted one lying in a bleached gray pile across an abandoned field. Bent Lake was one more hour up. I arrived just before sunset.

It was a one-block town, anchored at the front by a Dairy Queen and the remains of a gas station. The DQ's parking lot was empty, though the red-and-white wood hut was lit up bright with yellow bug lights and looked ready for commerce.

The gas station across the street did not. Its pumps had been pulled and the only visible reminder of its heritage was an oval blue-and-white Pure Oil sign creaking from rusty chains on a pole. The young man working inside on an old truck didn't jerk up, startled, as I passed by, so I assumed the town was accustomed to some degree of traffic.

I drove slowly past storefronts that were boarded

up. The only light came from a Budweiser sign in a tavern window in the middle of the block.

A cluster of old, clapboard motel cottages was curled at the far end. Its sign read: 'Loons' Rest. Rooms $30.' The paint on the sign was fresher by a couple of decades than the white flakes peeling off the cottages. A new, shiny blue Ford F-150 pickup truck with a big chrome radiator and pimp lights on its roof was the only vehicle in the lot.

'Forty dollars for the night,' the woman behind the counter said as I jangled the bells above the door, coming in. She was wrinkled and her skin and hair were colored almost the same gray as the collapsed barns I'd passed, south of town.

'The sign outside says thirty.'

'Them's off-season rates.'

I cocked a thumb at the window looking out at the parking lot, empty except for the truck and the Porsche. 'Hasn't snowmobiling season just ended?'

'You from Illinois?'

'Does that matter?'

'I like to know how our clientele finds us.' She smiled, showing me where she needed dental work.

'In desperation,' I wanted to say but didn't. Loons' Rest was the only place around, it was getting dark, and it wasn't hard to imagine insects the size of antelope roaming the deserted old town. I pulled out my Visa card.

'No credit; cash,' she said.

'American currency OK?' I asked as I peeled off four tens.

'That'll be forty-four with tax,' she said.

I added four singles. 'Do you know where Arthur Lamm's place is?'

'Never heard of him.'

'Thank you,' I said.

'Illinoyance,' she muttered.

'Cheesehead,' I said, but only after I'd stepped outside and banged the door shut on the woman and the jangling bells.

It was all so very adult.

My room smelled of the same strong pine cleaner the Rivertown Health Center sloshed about when a tenant expired, and I wondered whether the weak, twenty-six-watt bulb hanging from the stained tile ceiling was meant to conceal as well. Even in the dim light, the knots on the knotty pine paneling appeared troublesome, and I thought it best not to look at them closely, for fear some weren't knots at all but rather shoe-heel marks on top of cockroach splats.

A tufted orange spread covered the mattress, and a disconnected gold pay box for a long-gone Magic Fingers electric bed massager was screwed to the headboard. It never boded well when the Magic Fingers fled a town. For sure I would only stay one night.

I sat on the bed to check my cell phone for messages. It had not rung. The reason was not that there had been no calls or texts. My display showed that no bars of service were available.

I left my duffel tightly zipped on the bed – in case any of the knots jumped off the wall paneling, frisky – and went out into the dusk

131

Across the street, several teenagers were running along the sidewalk, yelling as they raked broom handles under the ribs of the corrugated metal awnings of the vacant stores. The racket was deafening, reverberating along the deserted street as though monkeys were banging on pans. Every few seconds, shadowy things dropped from beneath the awnings, which set the teens to waving flashlights, jumping up and down, screaming and laughing with delight.

It made no sense. 'What are you doing?' I called across the street.

They stopped and stared at me. 'Stomping bats, a course,' one young girl, pretty in denim and a pale yellow jacket, yelled back.

'A course,' I shouted back. There were worse places to grow up in than Rivertown, I supposed.

I stepped into the center of the street, reasoning that bat splatter was less likely out there than on the sidewalks, and walked down to the neon Budweiser light. Three men in flannel shirts sat at the bar inside, jawing with a bartender who had a red beard.

'Can I get something to eat here?' I asked.

'Pickled eggs which I prepare special myself, and Slim Jims,' Red Beard said. 'Anything fancier, you got to go to the DQ.'

I told him I needed fancier, and would be back for a brew after I'd eaten.

The Dairy Queen's parking lot was still empty, since the town's evening merriment remained underway beneath the metal awnings at the other end of the block. Inside the hut, a teenaged boy 'nd girl were pressed together as tight as a double-dip of soft-serve ice cream jammed hard in a cake cone. The girl saw me appear in the glow of the yellow bug lights and broke the clinch. So long as I only wanted a hamburger, they could serve me dinner, she allowed. I asked what if I wanted two? That froze her face until I said I was making a joke. They both smiled then, sort of, though I suspected they'd discuss it later. No matter. Two hamburgers soon appeared, and I ate them with fries and a chocolate shake at a picnic table facing the road, so I could watch the cars that passed by. There were none. Afterward, I gave them back their plastic tray and walked down to the tavern.

The three flannel shirts and Red Beard stopped talking when I came in. I ordered a beer.

'Up here for some early fishing?' the bartender asked, skimming the head off the beer.

'At Arthur Lamm's camp. Know him?'

The six eyes above the three flannel shirts turned to look at me directly.

'I don't think he's around,' the bartender said.

I put on my confused face which, in truth, is never far away. 'I came up from Chicago a day early. I hope I didn't get the date mixed up.'

'Lamm's car is there, but no one has seen him,' the bartender said.

'Does anyone know where he's gone?'

'Herman says Lamm's off camping. It's caused a ruckus. You guys from Illinois . . .' The bartender's lower lip curled down, following the thought that was dropping away.

I bought beers for the men at the bar, the bartender, and another for myself. It set me back four bucks, not counting the single I left on the counter. It made everyone more talkative.

'Us guys from Illinois, you were saying?' I asked.

'Cops,' the bartender said.

'There was only the one,' said one of the flannel shirts – his was red.

'Young sonofabitch,' said the man next to him. His flannel was green.

'What was he asking?'

'I didn't actually talk to him. I just heard he was up from Chicago, asking for Lamm.'

'Nobody knows exactly where Lamm is, and that includes Herman,' the third man at the bar said, speaking for the first time. His flannel shirt was plaid, half red, half green, which I supposed made him an excellent arbiter for the other two. 'And if Herman's been drinking, he wouldn't have noticed Lamm being abducted in an alien spaceship.'

'Herman works for Lamm?' I asked.

'Supposedly he takes care of Lamm's camp,' Green Flannel said, 'but Herman Canty's never done a lick of work in his life. Herman's what you call an opportunist. He latches on to things.'

'Like Wanda, over at Loons',' Red Flannel said. 'Latched on to that some long time ago.'

'Rockin' the cot, God help him,' Green Flannel said.

That got the three flannels and the bartender laughing.

'She even lets him stay nights, sometimes, when his sister throws him out,' Red Flannel said.

'Not all nights. She's not all dumb,' the

bartender said. 'She knows Herman for what he is.'

'A damned user,' Red Flannel said. 'Strikes at every opportunity.'

'This Canty, he latched on to Lamm as well?' I asked.

'Big time,' Green Flannel said. 'Sooner than later, you'll see a new blue F-One Fifty over to Loons'. That's Herman's truck. No one can figure out what he done for it, being as he's never been useful.'

'That truck come out of Chicago, according to the license plate frame,' Green Flannel said. 'He didn't buy it up here.'

'Either somebody died, leaving him an inheritance,' the plaid man said, 'or he's got Mr Lamm paying him way too large for watching his camp.'

The bartender was giving me a long look. 'You say you're a friend of Lamm's, yet you didn't call ahead to say you were coming up?'

'I'm more like an insurance client,' I said, 'but you're right. It's been a couple of months since he invited me. I should have checked before I drove up.'

'Cell phones don't always work up here, anyway,' the bartender said, shrugging. 'We're just yakking; nobody up here knows Lamm. He's certainly been too good to set foot in here.' He gestured at the murky shapes in the cloudy jar on the bar, as if to suggest that the eggs should have been reason enough to lure Lamm in. As if to warn me to not suffer the same loss, he slid the jar closer to me.

135

I resisted, saying it might incite the milk shake resting heavily on the hamburgers in my stomach, and asked for directions to Lamm's camp.

The bartender drew a map on a cocktail napkin. 'Mind that rickety old bridge on County M. It's a one-laner. Hit it wrong, you'll end up wet. And dead.'

I told them that if Lamm had indeed disappeared, I might want to speak to the sheriff. That got me another cocktail napkin map, and I left them to their pickled eggs and their flannel.

Outside, I envied their flannel. The night had turned frigid, and my pea coat was in Leo's Porsche. I hurried down the center of the street, deserted now, squinting for glints on the dark pavement. Nothing sparkled, freshly splattered, and I got to Loons' with shoes as dry as when I'd set out.

The inside of my cabin was as cold as the air outside. I spent five minutes looking for a thermostat before I realized that the cabin simply had no heat. I took a fast shower with what little lukewarm water could be coaxed from the pipes, dried myself with a towel that had a fist-sized hole in its center, bundled back into my clothes and pea coat, and slipped into bed.

I thought, then, of the newness of Jenny, waiting to warm me in San Francisco. And I thought of Amanda, and the easy, familiar way she'd warmed me, leaning against me in the Jeep, outside her father's house.

I tried to push those thoughts away, finding it easier to think about what I didn't understand about Arthur Lamm, the dead men in the heavy cream, and the frigid air inside the cabin. It wasn't until the middle of the night that I was finally able to shiver and shake myself to sleep.

Twenty-Seven

'I'm in real need of caffeine,' I said to gray-skinned Wanda as I looked around the motel office for the coffee maker. It was six-thirty the next morning.

'DQ,' she said.

I pasted on the best smile I could offer to such a creature. 'You don't have coffee for guests?'

'DQ does egg sandwiches. You could have a whole breakfast.'

'With ice cream, just the thing for a cold morning.' I turned for the door.

'You checking out?'

'I'll be gone by the end of the morning. Check-out is noon?'

'Eight-thirty in season.'

I looked out the window. The Porsche was the only car parked on the gravel lot.

'I imagine you need to hustle to get rooms ready for the next onslaught of visitors,' I said.

'Eight-thirty,' she said.

'I'll leave the key in the room for when you come to make sure I didn't steal either the towel or the hole in the middle of it.'

'Illinoyance,' she muttered as I went outside.

'Cheesehead,' I muttered back, but likely she

hadn't heard me, since I'd already slammed the door.

A truck shot from a parking space down the street and sped away. The truck was shiny and blue and I was fairly certain it was the one I'd seen in Loons' lot the previous evening, which meant it belonged to Herman Canty, Lamm's caretaker. If the rumors were true, that he spent his nights at the frigid Loons' Rest, curled beside the gray-faced Wanda, the man was entitled to whatever haste he needed to get away.

I drove down to the DQ. It was closed, though the sign said it was supposed to have opened at six, almost an hour earlier. I wasn't going to wait for someone to show up. I was anxious to speed out of that town, too. Besides, risking a launch of coffee in Leo's meticulously maintained Porsche, as I so often did in my Jeep, was unthinkable. I drove on.

Fifteen minutes later, in the sheriff's office, I regretted not waiting at the DQ. A massive caffeine-withdrawal headache had blossomed, and was pulsing along in perfect rhythm with the slow, doubting drone of the deputy sitting with his feet up on a brown steel desk.

'Tell me again why you're interested in Mr Lamm.' The man's tan shirt was stretched taut across his ample stomach, as though he'd often visited the DQ in Bent Lake.

'He invited me up for some fishing.'

His face was too red, too early in the year, to have come from the sun, and I guessed that his shirt might have been tightened more from beer than soft-serve ice cream. He craned his neck to look outside the window at the Porsche. 'Don't see gear,' he said, like he could see inside the trunk along with being able to smell a lie.

'Arthur said I could use his.'

The deputy sighed and shifted in the chair. 'Nobody seems to know where Mr Lamm has gotten himself to. People from his office in Chicago called up to report him missing. I sent two guys out for a day in a boat, and even hired a Cessna for an hour, but we found no sight of him. Then that damned fool Herman Canty up and says Lamm likes to go camping around this time of year. Wish to hell he'd spoke up before we hired a plane.'

'Lamm's family says it's normal for him to be camping for so long?'

'He's divorced, no kids. Ex-wife's out in California, and doesn't much give a damn. She got an annuity out of him instead of monthly income.'

'I heard a Chicago cop was up here looking for him.'

'Some kid, I heard, but he didn't bother to check in with me.'

'Lamm doesn't have a cell phone?'

'I tried. His was switched off.'

'How would I find Herman Canty?'

'Hard to say, especially now that he's getting about in that fancy new truck.' The deputy tilted forward to sit upright. 'You want to ask him about fishing?'

'I want to ask him about Lamm.'

'Herman will tell you Lamm's out fishing for muskies,' he said. 'Ever fish for muskies?'

139

'No.'

'Then what are you fishing for up here, Mr Elstrom?' he asked.

'Something I can sink a hook into, I suppose,' I said, and left.

Twenty-Eight

I followed the bartender's napkin map down roads designated with alphabet letters to junctions with roads marked with other letters, and finally came to the bridge on County M that the bartender had warned me about. It was a rickety, single-lane contraption of bleached wood and rusted brackets that looked to be spanning the narrow frothing river below more from habit than any lingering structural integrity. The bartender said the knee-high side rails were loose and the whole thing suffered dry rot. I took his concern seriously, and eased forward in first gear. Even barely crawling, the old planks shifted and rattled loudly, like I was disturbing old bones.

A fire lane had been cut into the woods one mile farther on. A half-mile after that, an eight-inch white board, with 'Lamm' written on it, was nailed to a tree beside two narrow clay ruts heading into the trees. I followed them to a clearing.

Herman Canty's shiny blue pickup truck was parked beside a dark Mercedes 500 series sedan made opaque from a rain-pocked mixture of dirt and bird droppings. I parked the Porsche and got out.

The log cottage facing the lake looked right for a rich man wanting to pass as poor. The timbers were splotched with moss, the black tarpaper roof was curling at the bottom, and green paint was flaking off the door and window facing the parking area. There was no lawn, just weeds in abundance, some two feet tall.

Capping the rusticity of the entire enterprise was a privy set far enough into the woods to provide splendid opportunities, while enthroned, for the intimate study of thousands of insects. I would have visited such a privy only under extreme distress, and then at warp speed.

The Mercedes was locked. I'd just begun rubbing the grime off the driver's window when a man stepped out of the cottage. He was lean, tall and grizzled with unkempt gray hair and a week's worth of unshaved beard stubble. Without doubt, he was tough enough to get through every word of the entire Sunday *New York Times* in the privy in the woods. Assuming, of course, that the man knew how to read.

'Herman?' I asked.

'Yep.'

'I came up to see Mr Lamm, but I understand he's not here.'

'Yep.'

'People from his Chicago office reported him missing?'

'Yep.'

For sure, the man must have enjoyed old cowboy movies.

141

'You told the sheriff there's no need for worry because Arthur takes off sometimes, for days on end, to go camping and fishing?'

He said nothing.

'That's a yep?'

'Yep,' he said. 'His business friends called me over at Loons'. Told them the same thing.'

'You didn't know he'd come up until you saw his car? You didn't actually see him?'

He stared off into the woods. 'Mr Lamm likes to take off, is all.'

I looked past him, toward the lake. An orange rowboat, barely floating above the waterline, was tied to a collapsing dock. 'Lamm's boat is still there.'

'Huh?'

'How can Lamm be off camping if his boat is still here?'

He blinked rapidly and licked his lips. After a minute, he said, 'He has two.'

'Mind if I look around?'

There was nothing friendly about the way he was now looking at me. 'What are you doing here, mister?'

'Arthur told me to come up any time for the fishing.'

Herman spat into the clay. 'Sure he did.'

I started walking toward the lake. Herman bird-dogged me from ten paces behind like he was worried I was going to make off with one of the trees.

When I got to the dock, I pointed at the boat. Barely two inches rode above the water. 'You're sure Arthur took a boat like this one?'

'Yep.'

'Must have bailed it out first.'

He spat again. 'I imagine.'

'Why didn't he bail out this one while he was at it?'

Herman shrugged. 'He only needed the one.'

'You're the caretaker here, right?'

'I look after things.'

'Why haven't you bailed out the boat?'

He looked away again.

'When Arthur gets back, tell him I came up to drop a few worms,' I said. I felt his eyes on me all the way to the Porsche. I hadn't bothered to give him a name. More importantly, he hadn't bothered to ask for one, as though he never expected to talk to Lamm again.

I drove the half-mile to the fire lane and pulled far enough into the leafless trees to hope the Porsche would be hidden from the road. The day had warmed. I left my pea coat in the car and doubled back through the woods. I wanted another look at Lamm's camp without Herman's breath misting the back of my neck. I got within sight of the privy when the sound of a loud engine came rumbling low along County M.

The woods hid the vehicle, but I guessed it was a truck, shiny and new and blue. Herman Canty, the man who'd made sure I'd left Lamm's clearing knowing nothing more than when I arrived, was driving slowly, maybe searching into the trees to make sure I had gone.

I held my breath, straining to hear any easing of his gas pedal. The engine loped on, low and steady. He didn't slow at the fire lane and, in

143

another minute, the big-barreled exhaust had gone.

I ran the last yards through the trees and down to the shore. I could see no other cottages or clearings at Lamm's end of the lake, no places where someone could see me prowling around. Several channels split the shoreline across the lake, leading to other lakes.

I stepped onto the narrow dock. The orange rowboat shifted uneasily in the water. The next rain, even if it was light, would drop it to the bottom of the shallows.

I went up to the cottage. It had three windows at the front, facing the lake. The middle one was unlatched. I slid it open and slipped through.

There was one big room, furnished simply with two vinyl sofas, a couple of sturdy wood rockers, a table and four straight-back wood chairs. Two gray metal-frame cots were folded up in the corner. I imagined the sofas would pull out for extra sleeping. A small, butane cook stove stood next to a large, wood-burning heat stove. Burned-down candle stubs stuck in glass ash trays were set beside two lanterns on a shelf above the back window. There was no refrigerator because there was no electricity; a dented green metal cooler rested in the corner, ready for ice or chilled water from the lake.

I went back out the window and down to the shore. The almost-submerged orange wood boat still nagged. Unless it had a hole in it, Lamm should have bailed it when he was emptying the other. Or Herman, simply because that should have been his responsibility.

into my legs with iron fingers. I dropped under the water, doubled over to knead my knuckles into my right leg, then my left. The cramps dug back deeper, relentless in the frigid water.

Damned fool me. I was going to drown if I didn't get out of the water.

I kicked for the trees, flailing my arms at the water as the great electric curls of pain wrapped tighter and tighter around my calves. My hands as well began to cramp, too weak to do anything but slap at the water. Swallowing water, I went down.

Incredibly, a foot grazed the bottom. I pushed up, saw sky, disbelieving. I was still yards from shore, but I'd touched bottom. I wanted to laugh, for the mercy of it. I screamed instead. From the cramps twisting deep into my legs.

I half dog-paddled, half-stumbled to the narrow ribbon of slick moss at the shore and crawled out on my belly. I collapsed face down on to the mud, shivering, sucking in the cool musk of the shore with ragged breaths.

And cursing. I swore at everyone I could think of. I cursed wedge-headed, cheese-worshipping, damned-fool inbred hunters. And their mothers. And the women who ran places like Loons' Rest. And their broom-beating, bat-stomping offspring.

I cursed Arthur Lamm, who might simply have been off camping. I cursed the lead-headed Herman Canty, stoic Northwoodsman, for not telling me anything definitive.

But mostly, I cursed myself. I'd almost died, not from gunshot, but from drowning in stupid panic.

A branch hung low above my head. I reached up and pulled myself up to stand. My legs wobbled and then calmed under my weight. Breathing came easier. After a moment I dared to let go of the branch, and bent to retie my shoe laces, loosened and slimed by ten thousand years of decayed plants and fish.

I started into the trees. The damp rotting carpet of last year's leaves muffled my footfalls as I pushed my legs to move quicker. My hunter might still be in the woods, about to spray a last few thousand rounds into the trees before heading home.

Even stumbling fast, whole swarms of stinging insects found me, chilled wet meat, pulsing with blood – a smorgasbord of lake muck and sweat served up in a thick residue of fear. I didn't slow to learn if they were mosquitoes, flies or gnats. They all stung like they were on steroids. Everything liked to hunt up in those piney woods.

Sooner than I hoped, I caught a shimmer of bright yellow through a thinning in the trees. Leo's Porsche, designed for the autobahn, hunkered low on the scraped clay of the fire lane, as out of place in those woods as I was. I dipped my hand into the pocket of my jeans, came out with the keys. Water dribbled from the little electronic remote. I ran up to the edge of the fire lane.

And stopped.

The sloped nose of the sleek German car was too close to the ground. The right front tire was flat. As was the rear tire. I backed deeper into